MICHAEL SPANDAU

Inquiries and Book Orders should be addressed to:

Great Writers Media
Email: info@greatwritersmedia.com
Phone: 877-600-5469

ISBN: 978-1-960605-68-9 (sc)
ISBN: 978-1-960605-69-6 (ebk)

CHAPTER 1

Power of the Divine Devil.

"Enough out of you, you disrespectful divine devil BASTARD! To Hell with you grraahh!! To make certain you don't return, I'll seal your power and wipe your memory!" Roared a wrathful voice moments before a loud crash was heard in central Germany. It was a 14-year-old boy with shoulder-length brown hair and green eyes. He was unconscious and taken in by the family of a high-ranking member of the German Parliament. The boy's mind was now a blank slate from the fall, they could mold his behavior to whatever suited them. He became the perfectly behaved child, practically a doormat with manners and social graces. They named the boy Tenzin after a week of re-acclimation, they sent him to school.

Tenzin arrived at school, everything went well until it was time for lunch on the way to the cafeteria and he was stopped by some kids.

"Hey, freak! You're the kid who crash-landed right?" Asked a taller, bulkier student with a grin on his face. Tenzin continues and walks around them, the head of the group then grabs his arm pulling it, causing him to drop his tray. The other students laugh at Tenzin as he goes to drop down and pick it up. He did not get far, they were holding his arm and pulled back up.

"Please let me go," Tenzin said, gently trembling and still reaching for his spilled lunch.

"You look me in the eyes when you talk, monster!" The bigger student barks, gripping him tighter.

"I said please." Tenzin moaned, looking up at him with tears in his eyes.

"Oh look, he's crying. Since you asked so nicely, of course!" The bully yelled, wrenching his arm downward, sending Tenzin into his lunch on the ground. The bully then kicked Tenzin in the ribs, stepping on the back of his head grinding it into the mess on the floor. The group of students started laughing at Tenzin as they walked away. Tenzin continued with his day at school and went home to tell his adopted father what happened at school.

"Father, these kids were treating me like a monster." Cried Tenzin, from the side of a large door.

"Quiet with your incessant whining! I'm working, learn how to handle it yourself!" Tenzin's adopted father yelled from the other side of the door smashing his desk. This continued as a pattern for the next two years, the sadness in Tenzin growing by the day.

"Hey, FREAK DID YOU THINK YOU COULD DUCK ME FOREVER!" The bully barked, cutting off Tenzin in the hallway with nowhere else to go. Tenzin began to look around a deer in headlights as he gradually approached. The bully began pushing Tenzin, as the bully took forward Tenzin shoved back three. The agitated look on the bully's face curled up into a grin as he saw the panic take over Tenzin's. The two stopped, Tenzin's eyes widened, he turned and saw that they had reached the wall. The bully grabbed Tenzin by the collar and lifted him against the wall with his left hand, pulling back his right. Tenzin winced for a moment, while he started unloading on him. It went on for a minute, straight of right hands then he began to sweat something fierce. Huffing, the bully dropped Tenzin. A pair of tears streak down on Tenzin's face but they don't get to fall, they evaporate just past his cheeks leaving his face scarred. The bully, down to a knee trying to catch his breath in the face of the intense heat, sees the floor crack as Tenzin steps forward. The bully looks up through the saucers on his face, Tenzin's emerald irises appear to be glowing, illuminating the fresh scars on his otherwise pristine face. Tenzin takes another step forward revealing the charred shoe track. The bully then stumbled backward and began to run away.

"You've called me a freak for so long, for what? Because of how I got here, and now as I display the truly freakish power you run? NO! You've tortured me for years, you aren't going anywhere!" Tenzin roared, as he rushed forward, shattering the windows in the hallway and scorching the floor, rocking the building when he stopped to cut off the bully.

"F-fr-UH I MEAN TENZIN, I'm sorry w-w-w-what I did was wrong I know," The bully stuttered, sporadically looking around, panicking behind every twitch of his muscles.

"WRONG! You think it's nearly enough to describe what you've spent the last two years doing to me!" Tenzin cried, the floor behind him bursting into flames.

"Of course not! I know it was awful. Please forgive me." The bully begged, dropping to his knees.

"What was it you said the first time we met? YOU LOOK ME IN THE EYES WHEN YOU TALK! You move your head again, I'll turn your body to CHALK!" Tenzin barked, looking down and noticing the bully wasn't moving anymore. Tenzin knelt and picked the bully up by the hair, his teary eyes closed. The bully had passed out from heatstroke, dropped from Tenzin's hand, his hair had just burned to cinders, and Tenzin dropped to his knees. "NO NO NO! STOP YOU BASTARD FLAMES STOP!" Tenzin howled, but the raging flames only continued to grow as they engulfed the hall and everyone else who had come to see what happened along with the rest of the school building. "How do I stop these flames?" Tenzin cried, dropping to his knees and clutching his hair before a glowing white light pierced both the inferno and the clouds in the great beyond. "That's how," Tenzin said, exhaling, calmly revealing the glowing white eye mark on his forehead. Tenzin then spread his hands apart and clapped his hand at the speed of sound. A shockwave was released simultaneously, putting out all the flames. "All the answers are coming to me, is this...omniscience. Oh, Michael! You fucked up. You should have just killed me. Who am I kidding? We both know if you were capable, I'd be dead already. I just need a few moments to get everything I need. What a shame Mikey. That seal would work on almost anyone else but not me. I'm not anywhere near my best, but I can still fly." Tenzin said, letting out a sigh and taking off at Mach 12. After about half an hour Tenzin landed in the Grand Canyon, grapevine in hand he threw it thousands of feet up in the air before releasing all the flames he could muster which erupted from his body filling a quarter of the canyon. Tenzin raised his hand to catch the grapevine and cut his hand open. Tenzin then bit off one of the grapes and held it between his molars. He licked the blood coming off of his hand. "Oh, that's good," Tenzin said, as he reveled in pure satisfaction. His irises turned from that deep green to blood red. In his right eye, a black cross replaced his pupil, in his left a white upside-down cross also replaced that pupil, and a red aura then started pulsing from his body. The sudden change caused him to inadvertently bite down on the grape, snapping him back to his senses.

"Oh NO!" Exclaimed, the same wrathful voice from before. His heart dropped as he thought back to what was to him just a moment ago.

"Oh come on Mikey you busted me up over an hour ago and haven't kept up since," Tenzin said, wearing an arrogant grin.

"You're starting to get on my nerves, *if I only use a little more, God won't notice* you had this coming, you abominable hybrid!" Archangel Michael said, sick of Tobias.

"You're a joke," Tenzin said before being interrupted by an ax kick to the head. He started spinning like a buzz saw and was sent flying. Before he could go anywhere, dangerous Michael nailed him with a punch to the gut. As the punch landed it resulted in his fist being ground into Tobias stopping him and smoking.

"How do you like that Tobi," he said smugly. Tenzin then kneed him in the gut, causing Michael to bend down. Tenzin then balled him up and punted him away.

"You know full well it pisses me off to hear that, so as payback I'm going to use you to practice my footwork," Tenzin said, glaring at Michael, and he began kicking him around back and forth. Tenzin continued this for an hour straight. "You make a better ball than a fighter. I am surprised my uncle did not choose Gabriel over you."

"I'm warning you right now, stop mocking me!"

"Or what? You'll give me a half-decent massage,"

"This is your last warning."

"What was that? I couldn't hear you over with my hand across your face and back and all," Tenzin said, just after appearing inches away from him. Tenzin then began slapping him back and forth across the face and stopped at the tenth time.

"My Lord shouldn't notice if I use my full strength just long enough to end him." Michael thought, before erupting. "Enough out of you, disrespectful Divine Devil bastard! To Hell with you grrraahhh, and to make certain you don't return I'll seal your power and wipe your memory!" As he knocked Tobias down through the clouds.

"I'm back, HAAAAAA!" Tenzin roared, flames erupted from his body, filling the entire canyon transforming it into a chasm of molten rock.

"I should have just killed him from the start, I'm responsible for this monster now." the voice said, with a gulp.

"I'm stronger than I was before the fall!" Tenzin exclaimed, leaping up and rocking the Earth on his way up as he passed through the clouds. Seconds later, he was standing at a massive gate of gold, pearls, and other gems. Tenzin flew towards the gate and kicked it open. A tall blonde man with angel wings rushed Tenzin but was quickly stopped by the hand through the left side of his chest. "Oh hello there Michael, you saved me the time tracking you down. I've still got a free hand, say Michael you need wings to fly, don't you? Let's find out if you can fly with just one," Tenzin chuckled as he ripped Michael on right-wing off and turned it to ash. "I'm going to count down from five, and your heart is going to pop like a water balloon," Tenzin warned as he lifted his pointer finger against Michael's heart. "Five." His middle finger followed suit, "Four." then his ring finger. "Three." Followed by his pinky finger. "Two!" Finally his thumb. "One"

"Tobias NO!" Barked, a self-important voice belonging to a large figure obscured by bright light.

"Uncle, it feels euphoric to hear that name. But he tried to kill me, and you were nowhere to be found, but you were watching, you always are. So I'm going to return the favor in full. Also, you're not ending the world, I'm pumping the breaks on Revelations." Tobias explained, squeezing Michael's heart until it burst and ripping his blood-drenched hand from his chest.

"TOBIAS!" God, roared.

"SHUT UP! Ohhhhh cousin, we've got an archangel at the gate that could use your expertise." Tobias' voice stretched across all of Heaven. Tobias flew over to God and drew a smile on his face in Michael's blood. Tobias flew back, and flames consumed his arm up to the elbow before dissipating. A lanky man with long brown hair, blue eyes with a mustache and beard, wearing a long beige robe and sandals arrived at Heaven's gates.

"Tobias, I always knew it was a matter of time until you would cause problems," Jesus said, dropping down to his knees and placing one hand on Michael's head and the other on his chest not breaking his glare towards the Divine Devil.

"That is the nicest way you thought to put that, and if looks could kill, I'd be in a worse shape than Michael. Slowly now, you wouldn't want to risk putting multiple souls in a vessel as powerful as that one, he could end up stronger than God over there. Or stronger than me for once." Tobias said as Michael sat up, gasping for breath.

"Are you implying you are stronger than my father, the Almighty GOD?" Jesus asked, enraged as he flew up into Tobias' face.

"I'm not implying anything I'm simply stating it as fact, that I am stronger than God. He knows it too, he knows everything. I've never thought about how strong I was before. Now I have, so he knows and he's quaking in the boots that will always be just a tad too big for you to fill. I've lived in Heaven for what felt like way too long, you tried so hard to be him, some of the mortals down there are foolish enough to believe you're both the same person. He killed you, and you still show that devotion because you're ignorant of how fathers are supposed to act. So stop being all high and mighty understand your inferiority. Now get out of my face." Tobias responded before Jesus staggered backward, clutching his face.

"What did you do to me!?" Jesus asked, looking up, his face smoking.

"Oh, you annoyed me so much that my power flared up and burned you. I have more of it, it's a bit harder to control." Tobias replied, starting to fall. Tobias uses his All-Seeing Eye to find Lucifer on Earth. Tobias saw a blonde-haired red-eyed Jesus.

"What the hell?" Lucifer exclaimed, looking up to the black flame streaking through the sky. As Tobias approached his right hand he began to emit a pale white glow. He used his left to draw an upside-down cross attached to a right-side-up below it with a backward capital d on the left side of the upside-down cross and a capital D on the right side of the right-side-up cross in the left side of Lucifer's chest.

"Luci, give me a minute. I can't have my uncle and cousin blaming any more mortal bullshit on you. So, I'm sending you to Hell personally," He punched through the symbol on his chest with his glowing hand. Tobias ripped a wretched gray misty orb from Lucifer's heart. He then used his all-seeing eye again to find his way to Hell. Tobias began to fly down to Hell, "Wow travel is boring. If I could cut my way into places, things would happen way faster. As a matter of fact," he used his all-seeing eye to find out if such an object existed. "I'll look into that later," Tobias said, to himself as he arrived at the gates of Hell. He tossed the orb into the fiery lake and shot back up to Heaven.

"Tobias, back already?" Jesus questioned, apprehensive and leaning back slightly.

"Yeah, the funny thing about omniscience, it makes things a lot easier. Didn't take too long, no need to make a whole war out of it. So the second most important part of Revelations has been taken care of but you cousin, are the main event. Do you still plan on going down to earth?"

"O-Of course I do, I will follow through on my fathers' plan," Jesus said, with a big gulp from the back of his throat.

"Well if that's the case, let's speed things up a bit," Tobias responded, a massive grin on his face as if he was hoping for that answer. He then grabbed Jesus by the leg and dragged him down to Earth, the impact separated the two. Tobias rushed Jesus kicking his head clean off then pinning it to the ground with the sword of black flames that launched through it. The head turned to ash before Jesus' body kipped up kicking away Tobias in the process. The light then shone down upon Jesus as his head reformed. Tobias charged back at Jesus, kicking his legs, causing the anointed one to spin like a pinwheel slowing down only after being punched through the gut. Tobias then grabbed him by the legs and began to whip Jesus around like a set of battle ropes in the gym. After launching Jesus into the air Tobias roared a wall of flaming black swords. Just as Jesus was able to compose himself, his eyes turned to saucers as his head was taken off once again. God descended upon the battlefield. He stretched his arm out forward, a ball of light smaller than an atom appeared behind Tobias, and a sword went through the heart of Jesus. This continued in rapid succession as God began to faint. All that remained was one more sword, and Tobias was boiling he grabbed the last sword before crashing down onto Jesus, now coated in blood.

"HOW MANY TIMES DO I HAVE TO KILL YOU BEFORE YOU DIE?" Tobias howled, forcing the sword down towards Jesus. The sword suddenly stopped, it was God holding onto Tobias' wrist.

"That's enough Tobias, you proved your point earth will stay as it is, or at least I won't interfere with it any further. At least tell Jesus why you want Earth to be left as it is." God said, letting go of Tobias' wrist.

"Oh that's right, you already know. Well, cousin, not only is your bar for forgiveness incredibly fickle but very few mortals that you believe have earned their way into heaven without actually dying don't deserve it. Not only that they torture each other way more than Uncle's Smokey pond could ever dream of. I want humanity to suffer with itself for the rest of eternity. I could go back and live happily ever after, but that would be boring, and also I want to look into something. You chose this fight, you have to suffer the consequences even if you are drained right now, that should be nothing for you, so go ahead and heal me." Tobias demanded, sitting down and crossing his legs. Jesus then stood up catching his breath, and held his hands over Tobias' head, Tobias was surrounded by a green glow and his wounds began to close. Tobias quickly keeled over and writhe in pain.

"You may be a Divine Devil but a devil you still are." Jesus declared as the green glow surrounding Tobias increased in intensity.

"It may hurt like hell but you're still healing me dumbass," Tobias responded, letting off a small plume of black flames. Jesus was sent reeling back. Jesus then created a sword of white light in his hand but God put his arm out in front of him. Tobias then stood up before winking at the two and jumping up to Heaven as a show of dominance.

CHAPTER 2

Ascalon Black Flame Dimension Cutter

"Oh, Azzy I know you can hear me, where are you?" Tobias called out, with mischief in his voice.

"You freak, if you won't play with me I will kill you in an instant. I won't hesitate to take your soul. I'd be doing everyone a favor." Azrael responded, annoyed, holding his hand at Tobias' chest.

"You can try, I wouldn't mind dying. I'd rather not but give it your best shot anyway." Tobias responded, straightening his body and putting his arms out to the side crucifixion-style.

"And now YOU MOCK HIS SON!" Azrael exploded, reaching through Tobias' chest.

"What'd ya know, still kicking," Tobias said, grinning ear to ear, he put his arms back down. Azrael, confused, starts tightening and waving around his hand in Tobias' chest.

"What is HAPPENING? I CAN SEE YOUR SOUL, IT'S FLOATING ABOVE MY HAND RIGHT HERE." Azrael screamed, his voice trembling

"I guess I am a freak, hilarious you have one job and you can't do it to me. Uncle's not omnipotent or even omniscient, he doesn't have infinite power he is just good at using it. To explain his false omniscience, he has two basic abilities the All-Seeing Eye which allows the user to see anywhere that any eyes have been before. The All-Knowing Mind gives the user access to any information the user desires as long as it's taken the form of a thought in thought-form. He's a fraud, sure he might be stronger than everyone else in heaven so I guess you and every mortal could call him almighty. I was essentially born with every bit of power I have right now. Think of it like this, if a mortal lives an average life they could lift 170 pounds through working, moving, and physical effort, the strongest mortals on the planet can do around seven times that. If you apply this logic to me at the most basic level, I could rip the planet's largest mountain from the ground and knock the Earth around like a rubber ball. But enough about my theoretical power, take me to hades." Tobias ordered, putting his arm on Azrael's shoulder. Azrael just stood there for a moment until he came to his senses. The two then began to vibrate until they seemed to fade out of existence. They reappeared in a foggy wasteland full of billions of small floating lights. There was no movement in the vast expanse. The only thing that stood out was a plateau in the distance. Azrael started covering his eyes from the same plateau.

"It's blinding like the first time I looked at God after getting domain over souls."

"Of course, there are souls everywhere. It's like looking directly into the sun for you." Tobias said, the light surrounding his hand, and he began knocking around the souls.

"No, the plateau there's one bright soul on the plateau," Azrael clarified, as he finished talking, Tobias bent down forward. With a massive gust of wind, Tobias was on the plateau. "Hades is just a bit bigger than Earth and cleared half of it in an instant," Azrael exclaimed, jaw practically on the floor.

"Ascalon Black Flame Dimension Cutter!" Tobias said as he wrapped both of his hands around the sword handle. Everything began to tremble as Tobias drew the sword, but it wasn't budging. Slowly the sword move upward, cracks started forming in the blade. He exerted himself more, and the fog rapidly turned into steam. With a roar, Tobias pulled out a deformed black blade.

"The soul was in the sword, but it's dimmed a bit," Azrael said, lowering his arm.

"What do you mean a soul IN the sword?" Tobias asked, having already returned.

"Souls are strange, when a body dies, the soul leaves, so typically it is my job to bring them wherever God designates them to go, but even I miss a few now and then. Sentient bodies are odd with nearly ever-changing minds and hearts, that's why souls can be taken from and given to them so easily. So if a soul enters an object, it's much easier for it to stay there but it's also easier to stay there, more likely that the soul will link to the object." Azrael explained, watching Tobias swing around Ascalon.

"Thanks for the lesson about souls mechanics, the only being in the universe without a soul I'll be sure to keep note of that," Tobias said, raising the sword.

"What are you doing?" Azrael asked, worried, stepping back a bit.

"Dimension Cutter!" Tobias called out, he slashed the air, creating a portal to Heaven. Tobias flew through it and appeared before God. God saw Tobias with the deformed blade and began to weep. Tobias was taken aback for a moment, but his shock quickly turned to anger. "You watch everything that goes on down there without as much as the twitch of an eyebrow. But you see me with this blade and have the nerve to BREAKDOWN INTO TEARS, I ought to kill you right now, and I could do it with a single slice. I have other plans at the moment though," Tobias barked, turning and slashing open another portal. "Dimension Cutter." He called out before flying through the portal.

CHAPTER 3

Eyes for Harmonia.

Tobias stepped onto a beautiful marble floor, upon looking up and around he found himself in a hallway. He was surrounded by artisan pillars and columns, beyond them seemed to be a large waterfall leading into a crystal clear lake and a lush green forest clearing.

"Who are you intruder?!" A woman's voice rang, strong.

"Don't you know it's polite to give your name first," Tobias said, with a chuckle as black flames consumed him. As he turned around his flames extinguished, as he saw a blonde-haired blue-eyed Goddess whose beauty to him was beyond description.

"Well, I'd hate to be impolite to someone who just attempted to intimidate me, my name is Harmonia. I am the daughter of Ares, the Greek God of War, and Aphrodite, the Greek Goddess of Love. Harmonia declared, extending her hand out for a handshake.

"I am Tobias, the one and only Divine Devil," Tobias responded, shaking her hand.

"It's not much of a pantheon, but if you're gonna twist my arm," Tobias said, before zoning out to the feeling of Harmonia's pulse.

"HARMONIA!!" Interrupted, an obnoxious voice. Tobias quickly snapped back to his senses and threw Ascalon at the buff large bearded man the obnoxious voice came from. Before the sword got halfway to its destination Harmonia had kicked the blade back to the feet of Tobias.

"That's my father Tobias!" Harmonia snapped at him.

"I knew that before I threw it, wait you were worried for his life. You're stronger than him! You're stronger than me!" Tobias declared, breaking out into laughter. Ares crashed down to the ground confused as to what just happened and how Harmonia was in the air now.

"Harmonia, who is this?" Ares asked, fuming as a war ax appeared in his right hand.

"Someone you don't want to provoke, attempt to harm me, I'll destroy the false sense of power you 'higher' gods of the pantheon have. I came here for some new threads and a scabbard for the most powerful weapon in history. I guess I'm getting a fight too, how fun." Tobias said, wrapping his left hand around the handle of Ascalon.

"We both know you don't need that Tobias," Harmonia said, descending to the ground.

"Fine, I'm yours now after all," Tobias responded, raising Harmonia's eyebrows.

"YOU WHAT!" Ares barked, swinging his ax. The impact created a vacuum rocking Mount Olympus.

"If you want me, that is?" Tobias questioned, not breaking eye contact with Ares.

"That strike would have split the largest volcano on Earth and all the lava inside clean in half!" Ares exclaimed, stepping back.

"I'll even be merciful and defeat your father without touching him," Tobias said, with a big grin.

"Oh, you're trying to impress me?" Harmonia asked, playfully.

"Of course not, if that were the case he and Zeus would be tied together by their beards at this point. Just wasn't sure where exactly you two stood." Tobias responded, looking up at the cracks slowly forming in the ax head.

"He's a neglectful, brutish, controlling ape. But he's my father and I still love him so leave him alive." Harmonia explained as a grin stretched across her face. Tobias tilted his head for a moment before licking his chops.

"Medium or well done?" Tobias asked, this time speaking to Ares.

"There's no way you can beat me without a weapon, let alone without touching me," Ares said, slowly stumbling back.

"Medium it is, the more you move the more it will hurt," Tobias warned, as the air turned to fire around him and expanded. Ares was consumed, he dropped to the ground and began rolling around. He was writhing in pain so intensely he shook the mountain and mortals in Greece could hear him.

"I surrender! By Zeus, I surrender, make it stop please!" Ares pleaded. Tobias waited two minutes before pulling Ascalon from the ground.

"What are you doing?" Harmonia asked, apprehensively.

"Putting him out, unless you want to throw him in the water, but that would only boil him. Ascalon: Flame Retrieval." Tobias called out, the black flames seemed to just disappear.

"That was sad. Probably the most brutal mercy I've ever seen. You said you're mine if I want you. Why do you want to be mine?" Harmonia asked, kicking Ares' smoking body in one of the pathways leading west.

"Although indescribable beauty is easily enough to suffice, it's actually because when I felt your heartbeat I finally felt like I could slow down. For the first time in my life, I felt truly calm, you're also the first person to understand what I'm truly capable of and not treat me as a monster or alienate me. I wouldn't dare think of calling you mine having just met you, but it is my choice to be yours." Tobias explained, with the first genuine smile he's ever had on his face.

"When did you feel my heartbeat," Harmonia asked, confused, attempting to avoid the important part of the answer Tobias just gave her.

"I picked up your pulse when we shook hands," Tobias responded, lifting his hair out of his eyes.

"Oh. You never did tell me what Pantheon you come from." Harmonia said, still wrapping her head around his answer to her earlier question.

"It's not technically a Pantheon because there's only one God but Judeo-Christianity," Tobias responded, with a hint of shame in his voice.

"Um, you'd probably know better than me but there are two Judeo-Christian Gods, the one mortals commonly refer to as Jahova or Yahweh and his brother, Gideon," Harmonia explained with a puzzled look on her face.

"I assure you there is and always has been one G-. Give me a moment." Tobias said, letting out a large exhale through his nose and closing his eyes. Harmonia stood and watched as a glowing white eye appeared on Tobias' forehead. A minute later his eyes burst open.

"What was that?" Harmonia asked, confused even further.

"I'm going to kill HIM! I'M GONNA KILL THEM BOTH." Tobias seethed, his voice trembling as a golden light began to fade in and out of his irises. Mount Olympus along with even Greece began to quake.

"Tobias, YOU HAVE TO STOP IF YOU KEEP THIS UP YOU'LL ERASE THE ENTIRE DIMENSION! PLEASE!" Harmonia pleaded, but to no avail. She rushed to Tobias, wrapping her arms around him and squeezing tightly, also raising her chin so it went as close to his ear as she could get it. The shaking stopped, and Tobias' eyes returned to normal, he then wrapped his arms around her as well.

"I'm sorry, I was just blaming them because they were the only ones I knew but when I found out it was their fault I'm like this I lost control. Harmonia put her palm on Tobias' forehead and her eyes turned into piercing lights. Moments later she let go of his head and her eyes returned to normal, a tear fell from her left eye and she kissed Tobias. After a moment of serene embrace, the two separated.

"Of course you're mine. Mine and mine alone. No one else could handle you." Harmonia said, she then grabbed his hand and they locked fingers.

"What was that?" Tobias asked, confused but happy.

"It's called a kiss, a lot of cultures view it as a sign of affection. What, did you think you were the only one with tricks? Forced Sympathy: it allows the user to peer into a moment of intense emotion and they see exactly what happened and how the other person felt in that emotion, it took me a bit to find what specifically you were talking about because all of your emotions are so raw. Almost essential for settling conflicts between particularly unreasonable mortals. Your turn." Harmonia explained as she led him north.

"The All-Seeing Eye: All-Knowing, It gives me access to any piece of information as long as it's taken the form of a thought," Tobias explained, tapping his forehead with his index finger.

"So you can read minds." Harmonia blurted, sounding excited and worried at the same time.

"No mind-reading is limited by having to be in real-time, imagine EVERY THOUGHT being in an encyclopedia, I can flip to the right page I need and read exactly what I want in an instant." Tobias clarified, looking around as Harmonia continued to lead him.

"You can't have only come here for new clothes and a scabbard for your sword, why are you here?" Harmonia asked, looking up at Tobias.

"That's a secret, but seriously where are you taking me?" Tobias asked, still following behind her.

"You said you wanted new clothes, your blade can wait," Haromonia responded, as they stopped at a large wool-covered door.

"What is this?" Tobias asked, looking at the door bewildered.

"This is the workshop of the Greek Goddess of Clothing, Clotho." Harmonia explained, before pushing the doors open.

"Clotho!?" Tobias asked as he broke out laughing. A misty black thread then materialized and attached to his heart.

"She's also the spinner of the thread of fate," Harmonia said, wide-eyed as a raggedy-gray-haired but surprisingly beautiful and youthful-looking woman yanked on the thread only to see nothing follow it.

"What! That's impossible! I control the fate of every soul on this mountain and in Greece within the Mortal Realm. You should be dead." Clotho exclaimed, literally cut off from trying again by Tobias' glowing fingers.

"Yeah, my soul's kind of on the frits at the moment. Even the Judeo-Christian God's Angel of Death couldn't take my soul. If you want to kill me you have to do it the old-fashioned way. I do respect the chutzpah though, but to me, you're just a divine tailor." Tobias explained, walking into Clotho's workshop.

"Crucifix pose" Clotho ordered, putting her hands out in front of Tobias' chest. Tobias smirked before spreading his arms apart and standing straight up. Magic circles appeared around the arms, legs, head, and torso of Tobias before tracing his whole body. "Alright Harmonia, what do you want him to wear?" Clotho asked, turning to Harmonia.

"I can dress thank you," Tobias responded, ripping off his blazer.

"If that were true, you wouldn't have come to me. Besides, she's going to spend the longest time looking at you." Clotho remarked, turning to her spinning wheel.

"I want him in a long black hooded coat with a red fur collar, and a white shirt underneath. Also long white boots and black pants." Harmonia responded, scanning Tobias up and down with her eyes.

"The clothes need to be temperature proof. Put this on the back of the coat." Tobias requested, he cut a symbol into the wall an upside-down cross attached to a right-side-up below it with a backward capital d on the left side of the upside-down cross and a normal capital d on the right side of the right-side-up cross.

"As you wish," Cotho replied rolling her eyes, the wheel began to spin and glow she snapped her fingers. The magic circles traced Tobias once again and he was decked in the attire Harmonia had described. Tobias strutted out of the workshop, flying up. Harmonia followed him out to see what appeared to be a black sun in the Olympian sky, heat began to bounce off everything as the air trembled. The black flames surrounding Tobias retreated into Ascalon.

"Well let's sheathe that sword so we can have a conversation without accidentally threatening whoever we're talking to," Harmonia called out.

"Just making sure I got what I asked for, again you can lead the way," Tobias responded, slowly descending to the ground and extending his hand. Harmonia took his hand and the two began walking again.

"We're heading to a different part of the mountain for this one, Hephaestus was given his palace because of how large his workshop is," Harmonia explained, as she led him north.

"If that's the case shouldn't we just fly there?" Tobias asked, confused.

"It's probably better for us to keep a low profile. You just beat Ares without touching him, if we're lucky no one's found him yet. Yes, I'm the strongest on the mountain but I'm not the strongest in the pantheon. That honor goes to Heracles, he's about twice as strong as I am. Hermes is always sneaking around somewhere up here, his Winged Boots are the only item in the pantheon that allow for instant travel between realms without magic." Harmonia explained, grabbing his hand and squeezing it tightly.

"By the way, where did you kick Ares?" Tobias asked, the two left the main square and were now walking through a large forest.

"I kicked him to the outside of Asclepius' workshop, God of medicine."

"So, exactly how far away is this palace?" Tobias asked, looking around.

"100 miles that way," Harmonia responded, pointing west into the distance. Tobias attempted to bolt forward but didn't move at all. He turned back to see Harmonia grinning, feet firmly planted in what is now cracked ground.

"Oh, right." Tobias sighed, the air began to ripple around their locked hands.

"You can't burn me, Tobias," Harmonia responded, their hands started warming up and eventually sweating.

"I don't have to," Tobias responded, slipping his hand out of Harmonia's grip. Harmonia put her hands together and a magic circle formed in between them. As she pulled her hands apart a spear appeared in her right hand. Tobias had gotten a mile away before stomping hard, making a crater in the ground to stop himself from running neck first into the spearhead.

"I'm doing this to protect you, I am both willing and capable to drag you to Hephaestus if need be. Now we are going to continue to walk to his palace while keeping a low profile. Understand?" Harmonia warned. Tobias slowly and carefully nodded his head in agreement. The two continued to walk arm and arm for a few days until they arrived at the palace. It was a gargantuan steel castle with two bronze pillars on each side at the front, emitting plumes of billowing smoke. Easily over 500 feet tall and stretching back a mile it would be blinding to anyone on the mountain if it didn't block any sunlight that could reach it.

"So, all of this is his?" Tobias asked, marveling at the massive structure.

"Keep in mind, he once had to build an entire labyrinth in this palace." Harmonia clarified.

"It must be an oven in there," Tobias said, his eyes following the plumes of smoke.

"Don't worry about that, he's also the God of Fire," Harmonia assured him, Tobias rolled his eyes in response. The two finally looked down to the also huge entrance, there were two tungsten doors with an iron beam hanging off the front similar to that of a barn door. Tobias lifted the steel bar and threw it to the side before pushing the doors open. His eyebrows raised as a reaction to the lack of temperature change. The moment they walked through the door there was the constant banging of metal.

"So where is he?" Tobias asked, looking around.

"I don't know, but due to how your power manifests it won't be difficult to make him come to us. Flare your power as much as you can." Harmonia said, tying her long blonde hair back.

"If you insist," Tobias responded, stepping forward before letting out a deep breath and relaxing. Heat began to fill the palace as small flashes of black flames appeared and were extinguished as quickly as they appeared. This went on for about thirty seconds until the banging stopped and a very tall blonde-haired brown-eyed god came storming over to the two of them.

"STOP, stop, stop, stop, stop, STOP! What are you doing?!" The anxious god exclaimed as Tobias took Harmonia's hand once again.

"Ah, Hephaestus there you are," Harmonia said, with a satisfied grin on her face.

"I need you to make me a scabbard," Tobias demanded, pointing Ascalon at Hephaestus.

"I'VE GOT THOUSANDS!" Hephaestus exclaimed!"

"Oh no, I need a scabbard that can contain a sword with potentially infinite power," Tobias explained, turning Ascalon around. Hephaestus took hold of the blade holding it out sideways wrapping one hand around the handle and the other on the top flat of the blade. A magic circle then ran across Ascalon.

"No weapon can have infinite power...WHO MADE THIS?!" Hephaestus howled, dropping the sword out of fear.

"Gideon, brother of Yahweh of the Judeo-Christian Pantheon," Tobias responded, picking the sword up off the ground.

"It would take the power of every god on the mountain multiplied together to equal even a trillionth of this blade's potential. It still isn't quite infinite though. I'm going to need a drop of your blood to make it so the scabbard can grow with you so it can contain the sword's power." Hephaestus said as he tapped his foot on a panel on the floor and pulled out a large bleach white tree trunk and began to carve.

"Oh, I also want a cross on the scabbard to slot in with the one on my sword to create the symbol on the back of my coat,"

Tobias ordered, turning around and pointing to the symbol on his back. Hephaestus finished carving and held the scabbard out before Tobias, he poked himself in the finger with the tip of Ascalon and his blood dripped onto the scabbard. In a flash the scabbard was golden and radiant, then Hephaestus' magic circle scarred the scabbard with a black flame pattern and blackened the cross at the top. Tobias strapped the scabbard to his belt at his left side and sheathed Ascalon. He closed his eyes for a moment, with a brief glow on his forehead and a sonic boom Tobias was gone.

"ZEUS!" Harmonia exclaimed, her eyes now saucers she quickly followed him.

"You're never going to enter the Mortal Realm ever again, you hear me? I know how fragile pantheons are, so I won't hurt you. If you heed my warning." Tobias threatened, hand resting on the pommel of Ascalon. Harmonia arrived and just waited for Tobias to make a move.

"You insolent little!" Zeus growled, throwing a lightning bolt at Tobias, mere feet away. The lightning bolt was split in two and Ascalon was now drawn, another lightning bolt formed in Zeus' hand but was cut in half before he could throw it. This repeated another 29 times until Zeus' palm would only spark.

"Looks like you're out of juice, how inefficient. You're a sitting duck now, keep in mind you only got to throw one because I wasn't ready. I can both see and know everything so if you enter the Mortal Realm I'll know. So be a good little king, and stay on your throne. Dimension Cutter." Tobias says, turning and slashing open a portal.

CHAPTER 4

Conception of the Divine Devil

"You haven't eaten in over a month, you are the son of God, right? You can make food from anything, even the rocks that are EVERYWHERE!" Lucifer exclaimed, wearily annoyed.

"A man cannot live on bread alone, and they require him every last word as well," Jesus replied, calmly.

"Well if you're the son of God, go ahead and jump because He says so," Lucifer said, snapping his fingers before him and Jesus appeared at the top of the temple in Jerusalem. "He will command his angels to save you and catch you, he doesn't want you to break a leg," Lucifer spoke, with boredom.

"God also says, one must not dare Him," Jesus said, just as calm as before.

"Ugh, how about this," Lucifer said, snapping his fingers again before the two appeared on a ridiculously high mountain. "I offer you the world if you bow down and take me as your new God." Lucifer impatiently offered.

"For the last time like God says, BEGONE Lucifer! Our Lord God is the only one to be worshipped." Jesus snapped, turning his back to Lucifer.

"So be it, I give up. *Well, that didn't pan out but let's see what happens if we add a variable that wasn't supposed to come until much later.*" Lucifer thought to himself.

Nine months later a baby girl was born to a virgin in Aenon, Israel, who died shortly after giving birth. Michelle was this baby's name, as a way to mock the Archangel. Another woman found the crying baby hours later. Ten years passed by.

"Mama look at this!" Michelle exclaimed as she walked over to the woman who found her with a worm in her hand. She then put her other hand on top of it before lifting it. A butterfly then flew out of her hand.

"YOU CAN NEVER DO THAT AGAIN!" The woman screamed before slapping her hand.

"Okay, mommy." She said, sniffling, wiping her eyes.

Five more years passed, and the woman that found Michelle had died. She was walking the streets of Alexandrium when she saw a man whose leg had been cut open. She knelt, put her hands over the man's cut and it began to close with sizzling sounds.

"WITCH!" The man screamed as he ran away.

"W-what?" Michelle responded, and everyone turned to the girl and started rapidly throwing stones at her. The moment the stones made contact they started turning into bats. Michelle then started running away, tears flowing down her cheeks.

"You better run witch and never come back!" A man shouted, shaking his fist in the air.

"Why, why did they throw rocks at me? All I did was help that man, and he called me a witch. No, if I just keep helping people they have to treat me better eventually." Michelle said, feeling certain of herself. She then created a black sheep from the dirt and made a cloak from its wool. Michelle took the black cloak and wore it like a hood. She then left Alexandrium and started traveling south to Jerusalem. Walking for eleven hours through the day and night Michelle arrived with dawn in Ephraim. She rested behind a barn she found on the outskirts of the city. She woke up to the sound of a woman crying before standing and peering past the corner of the barn.

"We won't be able to pay our taxes if our crops don't start growing, what are we going to do honey?" Asked a woman in tears, hugging her husband tightly. *"I wonder if."* Michelle thought to herself before starting to whisper.

"Strike them blind," Michelle whispered looking at the couple.

"My eyes! I can't see." The man exclaimed in terror.

"I can't either." The woman responded, just as fearful. Michelle then walked over to their farm and touched the soil before wheat started springing up, she turned and began to whisper once again.

"Grant them sight," Michelle whispered as she walked further into the city.

"Dear look! The farm! The crops are already a pace tall and still growing!" The woman exclaimed wide-eyed, so astonished that she failed to notice the black figure walking away from them to be quickly eclipsed by the height of the crops.

Michelle made her way into the inner city. She saw 4 men preparing to stone a woman trembling and in tears. Michelle then walked over to the pile of rocks they'd amassed and laid her hand on one of the rocks, seconds before they all turned into butterflies and fluttered off. Shocked and afraid the men ran off screaming 'witch' similarly to before, the woman filled with relief bowed her head and thanked Michelle. Moments later the whole town had been gathering toward Michelle, it was a mob filled with fear and hatred. Michelle ran, she ran fast so fast she almost lost the mob chasing after her she'd reached the Jordan and didn't stop running but the mob stopped in their tracks. She continued forward and arrived at Sychor in another day. Michelle stopped to catch her breath turning dirt into grapes for food. After eating she made her way through the city before settling down somewhere, for an entire day after that she managed to avoid the commotion. Just for one day, however, the next morning Roman soldiers stormed the town in search of someone.

"Where is the witch in black?!" The soldiers barked.

"Who is this witch in black?" A man responded.

"She is a woman in a black wool cloak, who walked the Jordan to get here from Alexandrium. This is the most likely place she would be." The soldier explained.

"I saw a woman in a black cloak walking somewhere around there." Another man said, pointing in the general direction of the barn Michelle was sleeping behind the night before.

"Thank you, sir, we'll see your next month's taxes are reduced," The soldier responded before walking over to the barn with the others. Panicking about what to do Michelle tried attempted to flee quietly. One of the soldiers saw the movement of her cloak and made chase. "After her, she's there!" One of the guards exclaimed Michelle began to run. Moments later she was surrounded by soldiers and they were closing in.

"Bestow upon her wings greater than those of Michael himself," Commanded with divine power. Michelle then sprang angel wings whiter than the clouds on a clear day.

"What the hell, this witch has the wings of an angel. That doesn't make sense." A soldier said, perplexed and in awe.

"I don't know where these wings came from but I couldn't be more grateful for them," Michelle said sighing in relief. She then flew for about seven hours flying towards Jericho, then changed course for Jerusalem when she got above it to ensure that if they went after her she wouldn't be found. She was above Jerusalem and she saw 3 crosses and descended to the ground before the one in the center. "Why, why are people so horrible towards me all I'm trying to do is use my abilities to help people. How am I any different than him?"

"Because your abilities came from somewhere else, you being a woman plays a role in it too."??? Responded, with pity in his voice.

"Is this God?" Michelle asked, in confusion.

"No, I am Gideon. Brother of the one you know as God. If he'd noticed you you'd have been struck down on sight, but he's too busy setting things up for his plan. I've been watching you for a while now, let's get the most important information out of the way. You are an antichrist born of Immaculate Conception who killed your mother on the way out of the womb. The woman who raised you merely found you when you were born. You're lucky my brother didn't notice you in all that stuff you did he would have been livid. You know I have a proposition for you." Gideon said, generously.

"Processing all of that, but okay what's your proposition?" Michelle asked, in shock.

"My brother loves to tell mortals that he is perfect because he created the world, but as far as Gods go he isn't even in the top ten. There are many Gods, why he's clear to say he doesn't want mortals praying to them not that there aren't any. Simply because he created Earth and the human race he can control them, he should have learned with the whole Lucifer situation that isn't the case. After that he decided to conceive a child but because he felt he was that much higher than humans he didn't even do it the way he wanted it to be done. He simply sent it down to a woman's womb so it would develop as a human. The reason he wanted his "son" to be born a human was so that he could easily manipulate and control him. Therefore, by extension, he's able to strengthen and extend the belief that both of them are perfect. That's far from the truth though his perfect son has killed at least two people. I'm going off on a tangent, he believes his words are the only to live by and has the power to torture mortals who disagree and abuse them to do so. Then had a son to cover more ground. He isn't perfect and you are living breathing proof of that, I would like you to help me create a more convincing argument. The problem with Immaculate Conception is that the ceiling for the child's potential is cut off at the power of the father. So if I have a child with you the child's potential is limitless and it's almost guaranteed that when he matures he'll be stronger than Jesus, even my brother himself. In my child living the life he wants to and being more powerful than my brother or his sentient microphone, he will have been born within our pantheon and he will be unable to control him. That will be proof that his words mean as much as anyone else's and putting all the power in the world behind them won't change that. Nor will anyone else if I'm lucky. If my brother manages to kill us for it I have a plan to communicate with our son." Gideon went on.

"I owe you my life, but I guess it's more than fair to ask of me to give you another," Michelle responded, happily.

"If the child is born down there my brother might notice the air of holiness emitted from it. So it'll happen up here, he's so focused on specific areas of the Earth he won't notice if it happens up here." Gideon explained.

"Wait, are you saying up in Heaven?" Michelle asked, excitedly.

"Of course, there's nowhere else to go that's up where I'd be," Gideon remarked.

"Oh, okay how am I getting up there?" Michelle asked.

"Like this, just fly up. I opened a hole in Heaven that only those with your blood running through their veins can get through." Gideon said.

"Alright," Michelle responded as confused as she was compliant. Michelle flew up to the sky, moments later the clouds began to open and light-flooded through them as she ascended.

Nine months later in Heaven, a baby by the name of Tobias was born.

"I can't believe you would DO THIS!" God exclaimed, absolutely livid.

"So what if I did? What are you going to do about it? Have both of us been killed? Even if you killed the two of us, not even you could bring yourself to kill a baby. And if you did you would be the biggest hypocrite in the history of existence. Think about there isn't a single instance in this entire situation that isn't YOUR FAULT." Gideon roared, back.

"You're right I'm going to have you killed. What is wrong with you?" God asked.

"What's wrong with me is that you rule over everyone as if you and your child are perfect in that everything has to go your way. This was my proof that you're not even close. You're lucky I could've gone about it a completely different way." Gideon responded.

"Oh really? And what way is that?" God asked.

"I could've just turned Earth into another sun," Gideon said, he turned around and spread his arms out, and stood straight up.

"Goodbye, brother," God said. Azrael reached into Gideon's chest but after he pulled out his soul it zipped away and vanished. Time passes in Heaven.

"Enough out of you, you disrespectful divine devil bastard! To Hell with you grrraahhh, and to make certain you don't return I'll seal your power and wipe your memory!" erupted, a just voice.

CHAPTER 5

No Remorse for the Trickster
God of the Norse

Tobias turned around, slashed open a portal, and extended his hand for Harmonia. She hesitantly took his hand and they flew through the portal. They appeared in a large beautiful throne room before a tall elderly man in a robe, with gray hair and a long beard stretching to his knees with a bead at the end of it. The old man also only had one eye.

"All-father Odin, my name is Tobias. I am here to kill Loki. I'm going to stop Ragnarok because the mortals deserve to suffer from each other forever." Tobias declared, and Harmonia watched in horror of his ignorance.

"As determined as you are boy, you wouldn't stand a chance against Loki. Assuming you could find Loki which you can't because even I don't know what form he's taken right now, you wouldn't stand a chance against him. Loki would tear you apart only to keep you alive so he could cut you down piece by piece to feed you to Fenrir. I can tell just by looking that you went to Mount Olympus, that's one of Ares' daughters, you pounded your chest in front of a few pitiful 'Gods' they cowered and boosted your ego. I'll ALLOW you to remain in my kingdom, Asgard, and pursue Loki if you can satisfy Thor in combat." Odin said sternly, he tapped his staff on the ground twice and the doors burst open.

"You called father!" Responded, a mountain of a man clad in studded leather armor, with long vermillion hair and a matching large braided beard.

"Thor, this is Tobias. The young upstart wants to kill Loki, if he can entertain you on the battlefield I'll let him. I warn you he's extremely frail, even a casual swing of Mjolnir could kill him."

"That's the most powerful weapon in existence, Ascalon, the Black Flame Dimension Cutter. Or at least it could be the most powerful if it wasn't in the hands of such a pitiful..., YOU'RE NOT EVEN A GOD!" Thor barked, he turned away and walked out the doors.

"Harmonia, you're going to watch this one from inside. I'm sure the All-Father has some way to watch the battle. I'm going to leave his favorite child in a puddle of his blood if there's anything left at all when I'm done." Tobias seethed, as he moved his hair back out of his eyes, revealing his gilded radiant irises. Tobias took a step forward, with just that step he cleared 1000 miles of the nation-sized palace or he would've. There was a thunderous boom that reached the end of the universe even in the Mortal Realm, Tobias had gone headfirst into the wall that is Thor's back but Thor just continued walking. Gold Flames exploded from Tobias' feet, Thor now feeling it and even being pushed slightly lifted his foot off the ground and leaned on the other foot. Thor spun, pivoting, sending Tobias rocketing forward, Tobias unsheathed Ascalon forking into the ground instantly stopping himself. Thor himself leaped forward and ended up mere yards away from Tobias.

"To give you the slightest chance of survival I'll only be throwing Mjolnir at you because if I hit you with it you'd be a fine red paste," Thor claimed, he raised his 24-inch python of a right arm and lightning struck his palm, sending Tobias flying a mile away. The silver head of a hammer could be seen on top of his thumb and his index finger it was flat at the front and curved to a spike on the back. Tobias closed his eyes for a moment and when he opened them he saw a silver blur, breaking his arm at the shoulder.

"It took Odin nine years to understand the power of runes it took me less than nine seconds," Tobias called out, he then let out a mighty scream and took off his coat before carving a strange symbol into his broken arm. His arm instantly healed and the symbol with it, Tobias left forward blade first and the tip of Ascalon just slipped off of Thor. Tobias then continued slashing again and again but still to no avail, not even a scratch was left on Thor. Thor then booted him away, breaking all of his ribs on the right side. Tobias, mouth full of blood and even angrier than before, used his tongue to draw the same symbol on the roof of his mouth and was completely healed once again. Hopped up on so much adrenaline he couldn't taste his blood. Tobias took Ascalon and drew a different symbol but this time on both arms.

"Oh no, I have to stop him. He may KILL THOR!" Odin exclaimed, jumping up from his throne. Thor opened his hand and Mjolnir came flying into it, before Thor could tell what happened Tobias was in his face. Tobias grabbed Thor by the hair and threw him to the other side of Asgard before catching up to him and punting Thor into Yggdrasil, the world tree that connects all nine realms.

"AH! THAT ONE HURT!" Thor screamed, as he scanned his body and saw no wounds, Tobias then caught up to him.

"You entertained yet?" Tobias asked arrogantly, Thor then pushed himself off of Yggdrasil.

"You fool, you made yourself physically stronger and faster but you didn't get any more powerful at all. You're inflicting more pain but you aren't doing any more damage if anything you may be doing less than before which was barely anything, to begin with." Thor explained, opening his hand again.

"So you're telling me if I do this I win?" Tobias asked, with a chuckle.

"TOBIAS DON'T!" Odin screamed, in the distance, Tobias drew a different mark on Thor as Odin arrived Thor began to writhe in pain. Lightning began to shoot out of Thor's body in all directions, Odin was zipping all over the place while Tobias was just casually dodging it. One of the lightning bolts struck Yggdrsil and the branch that is Asgard was severed from the tree.

"Can I go after Loki?" Tobias asked, turning to a fearful Odin.

"MY SON IS DYING." Odin cried, looking at Tobias in horror.

"I'm aware. Can I go after Loki?" Tobias asked once again, he bit down through his thumb so it would start bleeding.

"Yes! Fine, just save Thor." Odin pleaded, making massive gusts of wind as he panted.

"You could do it yourself, but I guess you're just too busy panicking," Tobias said, flying up to Thor. He drew the same symbol on Thor's back as the one on his arms and the lightning stopped and Thor was unconscious. Tobias then stepped back over to Ascalon before whipping the runes off his arms and sheathing them. "Now what is Loki right now? He's himself? Where...he's on Odin's throne. HARMONIA!" Tobias roared, scared half to death he bolted back to Odin's palace. He arrived and saw Harmonia...mangled, hanging by her entrails from the mouth of a huge wolf even by the standards of the Frost Giants. Tobias' lungs bellowed before he bit down into his tongue, blood filled his mouth, and the gold light in his burst through the newly formed crosses that replaced his pupils. Tobias appeared by the head of the beast kicking it on the chin, it was already gone. "Dimension Cutter," The Divine Devil whispered, Ascalon drawn he flew through Heaven at a gnarly curve he returned to Asgard with a golden apple in his teeth plucked fresh from the tree of life. Tobias' pupils returned to normal and his irises glowed once again. Tobias took his time walking to the blood-drenched corpse of Harmonia held together by a thread of flesh, he knelt and drew two runes within an instant of one another. The first to bring Harmonia back to life, the second to completely restore her body. Seconds later she regained consciousness and Tobias pointed her to the portal, Harmonia hugged him tightly. "I'm sorry it's no use, I can't hear or feel your heart-beat over my own but for the first time, and my soul is awake. You need to go. I don't think I could bring you back from what's likely to happen next." Tobias warned desperately. Harmonia tilted her head up kissing Tobias and hugging him even tighter before turning and walking through the portal resolve in her eyes. Tobias walked forward as the portal closed behind him, his power gradually building with each step as he approached the palace. Tobias kicked in the door and a subtle tremble took over his body. When Tobias reached where Loki was supposed to be he saw his uncle, Yahweh but two green lights pierced the silhouette of his head.

"You must be Tobias," God said, as he stood up mere inches taller than Tobias.

"I am the Divine Devil, yes. I'd be dead if I weren't and so would you if I didn't know what that meant. You must WANT to die before Ragnarok, and after how easy Thor went down I thought about just taking your tongue but you've gone and thrown your life away." Tobias sighed, the trembling began to increase in violence.

"Oh, you don't like me in this form? I do have another in mind if you'd prefer?" God proposed.

"I don't know how you could piss me off with any other form more than that one. But by all means, take your best shot it's not my life on the line." Tobias said, starting to pant while holding himself.

"I have a lot of spare time on my hands Tobias, I often visit Midgard. I could be anyone down there even teachers ha aha ha ha ha." God's laugh echoed. His shape began to change; he got a touch shorter but quite a bit bulkier. It was the bully. Tobias looked at the bully and started belting out maniacal laughter. Looking up, he dropped to his knees and his arms went limp still cackling the very walls of the palace they were in began to melt. Moments later the palace was a mass of melted marble and the air vibrated as the heat began to spread rapidly even turning the air to plasma. The bully began to writhe in pain as his flesh turned to a crimson pile of mush. The heat wave reached

Yggdrasil and the heat burst into gilded flames, the flames traced the edge of Asgard and began rushing to the center. The pile of mush was overtaken by the flames and not even ashes were left, the flames fought to consume Tobias but it was as if there was a barrier protecting Tobias and producing more heat making the flames rise. The flames got to a certain point and couldn't go any higher and started to curve back downward pushing even harder on the barrier of heat surrounding the still laughing Tobias. Eventually, the flames broke through the barrier of heat burning Tobias bringing him back to his senses, he stood up letting out a cry of pain as his left arm was burnt up to the shoulder and his right leg to the knee. Tobias unsheathed Ascalon, raising it into the sky with one swift motion.

"ASCALON: FLAME RETRIEVAL," Tobias commanded, the beautiful golden flames instantly began to spiral almost drilling themselves into the rain guard of the sword, even moving at speeds that make the light look slow it took over an hour to draw in all of the fire. Tobias used Ascalon to carve the healing rune into his shoulder but nothing happened. "I guess since Asgard is now essentially just a mountain of ashes Runic Magic won't work anymore. Damn it, now I have to fix myself up the conventional way." Tobias said, slashing downward and flying through a portal to Heaven. Tobias flew up to God with a massive grin on his face making eye contact or at least attempting to.

"This POWER! Your soul has awoken HOW?!" God seethed, clenching his fist.

"Oh this is the first time I've seen you angry, you're fun like this. But here even to you, I'm a god now." Tobias said with a chuckle sheathing Ascalon, Jesus arrived at his father's side even angrier than him.

"How dare your wretched soul show itself? Azrael!" Jesus screamed. Azrael appeared to vibrate into existence in Heaven, hand glowing he dashed at the asymmetric Tobias but was cut off by the head of a spear at his neck.

"Uncle, cousin, this is Harmonia; Greek Goddess of Harmony and Concord, and proof that despite what you self-righteous bastards think even I can love. The most satisfying part of it all is she could kick my ass meaning even she can put you in your place if necessary. It's time for my soul to go back to sleep for now because yes it can make hundreds if not thousands of times stronger but here it's more of a liability than anything." Tobias explained, gently taking the hand of Harmonia and resting his thumb on her wrist and slowly the gold light faded from his eyes.

"Merely that woman's heartbeat can weaken you that much?" God exclaimed, Harmonia's eyebrows nearly pierced the heavens had heard that. Tobias broke out into laughter.

"Cousin I'd heal me quickly if I were you, you're going to have to turn uncle's throne into a bed if I can't stop her because by the time she's done with him even sitting will be painful," Tobias struggled to say in between his laughter, Jesus rushed over to Tobias. Tobias was surrounded by a thick green spear that quickly dissipated as his arm and leg were back, Jesus was stunned to see that Tobias was still smirking and hadn't so much as grit his teeth. "Harmonia, as much as I'd love to see you kick uncle through his gates we have more pressing issues than his ignorance," Tobias said stone-faced, reopening the portal to Asgard and flying through with her. The two set foot on the wasteland still smoking.

"Where are we?" Harmonia asked, looking around confused.

"Asgard, or what's left of it anyway," Tobias responded, eyes widening as he felt Harmonia's heart stop as he sheathed Ascalon.

"Nothing, there's nothing left," Harmonia exclaimed, holding her hand over her mouth.

"Harmonia wait, use Forced Sympathy. I can't explain myself so I just have to hope you understand." Tobias pleaded, dropping to his knees looking up into Harmonia's fearful eyes. Harmonia once again placed her palm on Tobias' forehead but this time her eyes only flashed with the white light of just an instant. Previously when she used Forced Sympathy it was like looking for a needle in a haystack, this time it was as simple as glancing at a flame that had already engulfed half of the said haystack.

"We have to stay here and keep this place a secret, if any other god except your uncle finds out about this a summit will be called and they will try to kill you. We'll live here, I'll blindfold Hephaestus and have him build us a house here. I'll even rip Gaia from the very Earth to make it less desolate." Harmonia explained sporadically, her eyes darting around as her mind raced.

"They couldn't kill me if they wanted to, or they wouldn't even try." Tobias boasted, happy to see the fear leave Harmonia's eyes.

"Tobias you're not invincible," Harmonia yelled back quickly.

"I know that, but after they see what I've done here they won't be so sure." Tobias clarified.

"Tobias they have Chronos; The God of Time, he has complete control over time if he wanted to he could completely rewind time in this entire dimension and bring back all of the Norse Gods with a vengeance!" Harmonia exclaimed.

"You saw what I did to Fenrir, even if Thor, Loki, and Odin all attacked at once they still might not be able to kill me like that. Besides, I did this on accident but they don't know that either. I'm not quite ready to go into hiding I have a political mess to clean up." Tobias responded, drawing Ascalon once again.

"What are you talking about politics, Yahweh hasn't been in contact with any other gods since shortly after the creation of Earth," Harmonia asked, surprised grabbing Tobias' wrist.

"The Plague of Egypt, he encroached on another pantheon's mortal territory. My father was in the middle of discussing reparations before he was killed because of my birth." Tobias responded annoyed.

"You don't seem like the diplomatic type Tobias," Harmonia said, sliding her hand over the cross on Ascalon's guard.

"I'm not, I'm going to scare them. As far they're concerned they were discussing what my father was going to do to make it up to them and then he just started ignoring them." Tobias explained, he raised Ascalon.

"Tobias! Hello! Greek Goddess of Harmony, I could resolve this problem within the hour." Harmonia exclaimed.

"Yeah but this is going to be more fun, if I'm lucky my soul will reawaken and I'll learn to handle all the power I released here," Tobias said, now grinning.

"But you're out of power." Harmonia shot back.

"Have you ever been in and out of the mortal realm, does strange things to the body? Dimension Cutter!" Tobias exclaimed, slicing downward and offering his hand to Harmonia once again. Harmonia took his hand and the two flew through the portal.

CHAPTER 6

The Eleventh Plague;
Wrath of the Divine Devil

The two came face to face up close and personal, before a muscular humanoid creature with the face of a Jackal. The portal closed as Tobias took a massive leap backward he then let go of Harmonia. They were now in a vast desert with a long winding river that cut through.

"You there your eyes show strength, your heart shows courage, and your mind shows fear. I shall judge your soul." The creature said, raising a scale to Tobias. The scale began to glow but then nothing, Tobias flicked the scale and chuckled.

"Sorry Anubis, I'm not going anywhere my soul's a bit too tired to step on the scale. Hell even if it was up, I doubt that scale would move an inch. I'm Tobias the Divine Devil, here on behalf of Gideon. And this…" Tobias stopped, he turned and lowered his hand out in front of Harmonia.

"We're already well acquainted, but I am engaged now," Harmonia said, taking Tobias' hand and kissing it.

"Pleasant news, of course, you'll hear no objections from me. I guess you already know each other makes sense the rest of the Olympians did retreat here during the war with the Titans." Tobias responded, grinning eyebrows raised.

"So Tobias, you're here to discuss reparations?" Anubis asked, opening his hand as the scale dissipated.

"No, I'm here to save us both time. I didn't want to risk turning Heaven to ash, I knew you were planning an invasion. I would have done all the fighting anyway, uncle and cousin wouldn't have lifted a finger, and the Archangels would have all died in the first five minutes." Tobias said, grimacing as he extended Ascalon at Anubis. Anubis' expression didn't change as he booted Tobias square in the gut, sending him flying ten feet back which would have been ten times further if Harmonia wasn't there to catch him. Tobias now with a mouth full of blood licked his chops and arched backward. His irises turned from that deep green to blood red. In his right eye, a black cross replaced his pupil, in his left a white upside-down cross also replaced that pupil, and a red aura then started pulsing from his body. Tobias spat out the blood with a smile on his face, the sand on the ground in that area turned to luscious soil.

"WHAT IS THAT? WHAT AM I HEARING?!" Anubis asked, stiffening up as his foot slid back.

"Oh is Hell a little scarier than where your dinghy takes the mortals with heavy souls? Trust me it is not as bad if you've been there, life as a mortal among mortals is much worse." Tobias laughed, he charged at Anubis's blade first. Anubis put his arms up, Tobias was there slashing downward but the blade just stopped dead on his wrist. Anubis was shocked to find he didn't feel any pain, he pushed back on the blade on it began to bow. Wide-eyed, Tobias sprang back and sheathed Ascalon.

"That sword is useless, why would you even fight with it?!" Anubis exclaimed.

"Ascalon is as powerful as the wielder," Tobias responded.

"You're pitifully weak then." Anubis shot back quickly.

"Don't think you can just stand around doing nothing!" A jackal-headed woman roared, as she dropped down above Harmonia, staff in hand one end was an ankh the other was a spearhead. Harmonia turned around grabbed the staff and broke it in half with a chop before kicking her away. A magic circle scanned down Harmonia's body and her hair was now up into two braided loops and she was holding a sword.

"Oh, hello Anput. I was hoping to see Tobias fight a battle that wasn't completely one-sided but oh well." Harmonia said, waiting as Anput bolted at her. She jacked Anput's jaw with the sword pommel, knocking her off balance. Harmonia dropped down tripping her and skewering her skull with her blade, she put on foot on Anput's stomach, gripped the handle tightly, and spun as if dancing tearing her head off her shoulders in the process. Tobias rushed at Anubis swiping at his arm, the arm faded into a ghostly image of itself and then returned. He then reached through Anubis' chest, the same thing happened again. Tobias then went at his face and his finger only touched it for it an instant before Anubis lept backward. The jackal face vanished revealing the face of an elderly dark-skinned man.

"I'll be damned, the jackal head was a mask, a powerful mask too. So are you going to surrender or," Tobias offered, before being interrupted?

"TOBIAS MOVE!" Harmonia warned, Tobias flew up just in time to see the Anput-kabob pierce Anubis' chest.

"I'd continue with my ultimatum but I don't think you want to live anymore." Tobias declared, Anubis screamed, dropping to his knees and a tear began to run down his face. Tobias placed his hand on top of Anubis's head. Anubis dissipated and Anput followed shortly after. Everything within the dimension began to rumble and a fearsome powerful voice spoke as Tobias and Harmonia tensed up as they began to be pulled toward something.

"You've killed two of my children and for that, you have incurred the wrath of Ra, Sun God and Patriarch of the Egyptian Pantheon." A falcon-headed behemoth of a god descended upon them. Tobias giggled and trembled as the crosses in his eyes once again burst into golden flames and his body relaxed. Ra raised his hand and in the sky far above them a star the size of Earth appeared. Tobias disappeared and seemed to take the star's place and even from the same distance felt hotter than the star that was just there. Tobias put his hands together and there was an explosion around him twice the radius to Earth due to the instant temperature but he was no longer giving off heat. With a sigh, Tobias dropped down mere inches from Ra and locked his fingers. He hit Ra with an Axe handle and he no longer existed, the sun in the Egyptian sky then permanently turned black. Tobias turned around and was greeted at the lips by Harmonia, the crosses faded back into his pupils and then they embraced. After a minute the gold light faded from Tobias' eyes and his soul slept once again.

"There isn't a single god or goddess alive capable of hurting me, let alone killing me when I'm like that. So if they somehow get more powerful than us, I can still protect you when it counts." Tobias said, fainting in Harmonia's arms with a smile on his face. Harmonia took Ascalon from his waist and carried him into the Ashes of Asgard, the smoke still not entirely clear.

CHAPTER 7

Divine Summit

"I've called this summit to discuss the balance of power in the Realm of the Gods." Zeus declared, his face contorted with disgust as he looked from the head onto an absurdly long table floating in a void containing a massive star in the distance with at least a hundred full chairs surrounding it. Each place at the table has a dark emerald-colored orb at it, Zeus' orb glowing as his hand rested on it. The two seats beside Zeus he were empty and so was the seat at the foot of the table. The orb began to pulse and Zeus removed his hand.

"Where are Odin, Ra, and Yahweh?" Asked a voice booming from the other end of the table. It was a dark-skinned god with curly dark hair and a long matching beard.

"That's the reason you're all here, Enlil. Odin is dead along with the rest of the Norse Gods and Ra probably met the same fate," Zeus responded, a bearded man wearing a helmet with wings on his head peered through a portal and whispered something to him. "WHAT!" Zeus barked, his eyes widened and he grits his teeth and slammed his fist on his table. He flipped a switch under the table and a small gray transparent model appeared floating in front of him. Zeus spun the model around and tapped on Egypt, zoomed in, and pushed it up into the air, it expanded for all the gods to see.

"So what, it's nighttime in Egypt?" Enlil questioned, his orb began to blink.

"There's no moon in the sky, its morning there the sun has blackened. I've been informed that Ra is dead, and he was killed by that insolent Divine Devil bastard. Tobias, son of the late Gideon and Yahweh's premature Antichrist is the reason I've called you all here. He wiped out the entire Norse Pantheon, turned Asgard to ash, threatened me, and as we all can see killed Ra. None of us can stop him, so I suggest we breed a champion from the strongest god and goddess from different pantheons. Yes, I fully understand we outlawed it for our safety but that was before the birth of a being who could erase entire pantheons in an instant." Zeus explained before his orb started to blink. A pale-skinned goddess with long black hair in a kimono put her hand on the orb in front of her.

"Without an all-out war, how do you suggest we prove who's the strongest?" She asked, removing her hand from the orb.

"Simple Amaturasu." Zeus responded, snapping his fingers as a magic circle appeared a foot and a half above the table and descended revealing Mjolnir and Thor's gauntlets.

"Where did you find those?" Enlil asked, hand on his orb.

"Those dwarves were damn good craftsmen, these were left in the Ashes of Asgard. I'm astounded they survived the destruction. So starting with the Greek Pantheon because we found it, every god and goddess from every pantheon will attempt to lift Mjolnir and the first of each to hoist it above their heads will produce a child together; our champion and the one that will restore balance to the Realm of the Gods. I've informed my pantheon already, in the meantime you can all inform yours." Zeus' voice echoed, as he took his hand off the orb. Zeus snapped his fingers once again, a magic circle descended behind him opening a portal. Ares stepped through and failed to pry so hard he ripped his own arms off on Mjolnir, then Hades, then Posideon, and so on not a single Greek god could get the hammer to budge.

"So, who's next?" asked Enlil.

"We're not done yet. My Kingdom may end with the gods but my pantheon does not." Zeus said, rolling his eyes. A large sandal stepped through the portal, you'd think the one that walked through was another Zeus but this man was a whole five feet taller than him.

"We're not waiting for you to set the other Titans free, this is already underhanded and it is your last chance, go ahead Kronos all the other Greek Gods failed pitifully!" Enlil exclaimed.

"I'm no god, I'll show you the difference between my power and theirs," Kronos said, stepping up onto the table. Kronos walked up to the hammer, reaching down with his right hand wrapping his fingers around the handle. He looked down focusing on the handle for a moment and a clock appeared in his right eye and he was able to lift the hammer as if it weighed nothing at all, he hoisted it above his head quickly shifting his focus to his hand. A lightning bolt struck the head of the hammer and Kronos dropped it and stepped down from the table.

"Now, it's time to decide who the mother of our champion will be and the Hindu Goddesses will go first because they have the most territory in the Mortal Realm behind Yahweh. Alright, Brahma, who is your first goddess?" Zeus asked, stroking his beard as he sat back and the portal behind him closed.

"Parvati or I guess more accurately Durga," Brahma responded, putting his sets of hands together and a portal opened behind him. A goddess with long black hair, tan skin, and ten arms walked through. The portal quickly closed behind her causing a look of shock to spread across the face of every god and goddess at the table like a virus. Durga stepped up onto the table and walked over to Mjolnir and wrapped four hands around the handle and the remaining six hands around those four wrists for further support. She began to lift the hammer and it left the ground managing to get it up to her head before her arms gave and it fell to the ground. Zeus put a hand on his orb but then it started blinking, he looked over to Brahma who had a finger in front of each of his mouths as if to shush him.

Durga's hair began to dance and her eyes glowed red before her head split and her body tore open. A radiant blue-skinned goddess burst out of Durga's forehead, with red piercing eyes and four arms, she wrapped all four around the handle of Mjolnir. Kali easily hoisted Mjolnir above her head as lightning struck the hammer, she turned and threw the hammer at Kronos. For a moment time stopped so Kronos could appropriately move his hand, to the others, it just appeared as if Kronos swatted Mjolnir down by its head sending it crashing into the ground.

"So I'm guessing she won't let me eat this one," Kronos said, smirking smugly.

"This champion is to live on Mt.Olympus because it's simply safer, there's nowhere the child could wander off to and have its soul stripped from its body or be reincarnated into a regular Hindu God or Goddess. No one would want all the work we put in to simply be reset would we and the child will wield Mjolnir. Furthermore, they will be raised by Ares and Athena. The conception will take place as soon as the summit is over, we need this child to be fighting fit as soon as possible. With that, I hereby conclude this summit." Zeus declared.

CHAPTER 8

Lover's Quarrel

Tobias' eyelids shuttered as he stirred in bed. He awoke, quickly sitting up and looking around to find himself in a large bed inside what appeared to be the bedroom of a log cabin. Tobias got out of bed and grabbed the sheathed Ascalon leaned against the nightstand clipping it onto his belt and put on his boots at the foot of the bed. He left the bedroom closing the door behind him and picked up the amazing aroma of something cooking and followed it to the kitchen where Harmonia was cooking up the perfect storm.

"Well look who rose from the dead," Harmonia remarked.

"Funny." Tobias scoffed, rolling his eyes and sitting down at a table with utensils placed at four places.

"If it makes you feel better you beat your cousin by a day." She responded.

"I've been out for two days!" Tobias exclaimed, Harmonia walked over and placed a bowl of some sort of bean soup in front of Tobias at the table. He ate a spoonful and his eyes turned into saucers, Tobias downed the broth and used the spoon to completely devour the solids.

"Clearly. You just ate like it was two years." Harmonia said, blushing.

"I lived in Heaven, ate from my vine, and had a status similar to that of royalty among the mortals, and ate golden apples from the Tree of Life. Yet that was far and away from the best thing I've ever eaten." Tobias declared, extending his bowl for seconds.

"My mother is the Goddess of Love and the quickest way to a man's heart is through his stomach, she's good for more than just the bedroom," Harmonia explained, filling the bowl up and handing it back to him. The second bowl has gone faster than the first once again extending it, but this time it was slightly pushed back.

"What? No more, that's cruel." Tobias said, genuinely disappointed.

"Save room I've got half a cow in the oven," Harmonia responded, opening the oven door.

"Isn't that a lot?" Tobias questioned.

"Not we have almost an unlimited supply of cattle because the mortals just kept sending them. Originally Zeus just wanted a few hundred for parties and weddings but I guess he forgot to account for the time difference between the realms." Harmonia explained.

"So you're saying every animal on Mt.Olympus was a sacrifice?" Tobias asked, with an eyebrow raised.

"Of course not all of them," Harmonia responded, hiding her uncertainty.

"Excuse me for just a moment," Tobias said, standing up and walking away from the table. Tobias used the All-Seeing Eye for about ten seconds, he drew Ascalon holding it out before him with his other hand at the tip. A magic circle scanned the blade and Tobias extended it in the direction of Harmonia but before it could get close it instantly shrank down to the size of a dagger.

"I'm sorry did you just instantly learn magic to turn your sword into a steak knife?" Harmonia asked, shocked and almost insulted.

"I picked up the basics and learned how to do exactly what I needed to do. Now I kind of regret the destruction of Asgard, Runes are a lot simpler; you draw the symbol and the effect triggers. Magic is a whole process with more rules and conditions than I care to learn, but I can do this." Tobias said, lifting his palm; creating a magic circle a flame appeared above it for a moment which turned into water, then into ice, a rock, a ball of wind, and a ball of light before the circle shrank and the light petered out. Tobias put the compacted Ascalon on the table next to his fork.

"Could you use the All-Seeing Eye to learn the abilities of other Gods and Goddesses?" Harmonia asked, turning around to pull a huge beef roast out of the oven.

"I would learn how they work, but I wouldn't automatically learn how to use them. I can't just close my eyes and get new powers, the simplest way to explain it is the moment you learned any magic whatsoever you could probably materialize weapons without being taught or at least after only seeing Ares do it once, but with the little magic I know," Tobias put his hands together and a magic circle appeared between them, he widely separated and opened his hands as if he was holding something. The magic circles split into two and spread apart creating the image of a bow staff and as the circles reached his fingertips each turned into a small puff of smoke and nothing happened. "Perhaps if I were smarter I could, All-Seeing just gives me the information how I apply it boils down to my intelligence," Tobias explained, pulling his chair out and sitting back down. Harmonia placed the beef roast on the table, the platter the roast rested on took up two-thirds of the table. Tobias grabbed his fork and the compacted Ascalon and was mere inches from carving into the steer's flesh. Harmomia slapped his hand away, sending the blade flying and pinning it to the wall.

"ARE YOU CRAZY?! You have to let it sit for at least five minutes, you could have flooded the whole table with the juices." Harmonia exclaimed, before gasping and covering her mouth as she saw Tobias grab his wrist and struggle to close his hand. Tobias blinked and his forehead flashed for a second, he got up and walked over to the wall pulling out and expanding Ascalon. He sheathed the blade, walking back to the hallway where the bedroom was. Tobias reached a door at the end of the hallway, he opened the door to a massive bathroom and was taken aback. There was a white tile floor, a huge bath letting off steam a hundred feet long and three feet deep with a green magic circle on the bath floor. Forty feet to the right there was a massive magic circle in the air generating a cloud that rained hot water. The walls were mirrors with magic circles that blew cool air closely lining the floor, Tobias looked to the inside of the door and saw his jacket on one of the hooks and took it. As he put on the jacket Tobias noticed the strong scent of Harmonia on it. Tobias walked back to the kitchen, entering as he unrolled the wrists on his jacket.

"We've got time to kill, I still feel a bit stiff follow me outside. Don't worry it won't get cold I just want to loosen up and have a little fun." Tobias said, turning the doorknob.

"Tobias wait I'm sorry, we don't have to do this." Harmonia pleaded, grabbing Tobias' hand.

"Why are you talking like that, I'm not mad. You just seem to have a lot of energy and you're out of your mind if you think I'm gonna sit here and watch that roast taunt me for five whole minutes." Tobias said, flying out of the doorway pulling Harmonia with him, and throwing her across the lush open field. A magic circle scanned Harmonia and her headband was in front of her now braided hair and she summoned a sword before charging at Tobias. Opening with an onslaught of slashes, Harmonia forces Tobias to take the defensive. Dodging all of the sword slashes Tobias kicks Harmonia in the stomach, he follows it up with a roundhouse to the head sending her flying away. Harmonia rebounding swings her sword at Tobias' feet, he jumps it creating a scar on the ground. She then charged him once more Tobias tries to get up but trips on the scarred ground behind him. Harmonia standing over Tobias the tip of her blade at his neck.

"Guess that means I win," Harmonia declared. Tobias, still with Ascalon in hand, ignites the blade nearly burning

Harmonia causing her to jump back. Tobias kipped up, extinguishing Ascalon. Finally going on the offensive he charged at Harmonia. Harmonia regained her composure, bracing herself for the oncoming Tobias. As Tobias got to her a magic circle was in his hand she put her arms up to block the incoming attack but it was just a blinding flash. Tobias hooked his feet on her bent arms flying up in a loop using the built-up force to slam Harmonia into the ground, following it up with a knee to the temple sending Harmonia flying back. Unscathed and now with her sight back Harmonia dusts herself off, she rushed Tobias picking up her sword on the way. Harmonia reaches Tobias, jacking him in the chin with the sword's pommel and sending him reeling with a punch square in the chest.

"This battle is over Tobias. I'm just as strong and way too fast for you. You. Can't. Beat. Me." Harmonia said, delivering a left kick, right kick, and a left punch and right punch as she spoke each word respectively, sending him back slightly.

"Who said I was trying to, you're your father's daughter but can back up what you say. Alright, I think it's been five minutes. You may have won this round, but this was just the first of many." Tobias said, sheathing Ascalon and stumbling back over to the door.

CHAPTER 9

Tipping the Scales

"I can't believe Zeus dropped his problems on us again. Seriously, he'll be lucky if I don't kill the child on accident the first time we spar." Ares protested, trembling with rage.

"If you don't want to raise the child that's fine, I'll do it myself. I can cover anything you would've and more, besides you've already been humiliated by the Divine Devil enough as it is I'd hate for the child to pick that up." Athena shot back, annoyed reaching for the whip at her hip. Ares snarled, putting his hands together materializing a hammer similar to Mjolnir and the gauntlet on Athena's left arm turned into a shield raising it to block the incoming hammer swing. Ares wound up to swing again but Athena used her whip to grab the hammer and throw it aside, knocking Ares to the ground with a shield strike. Athena cracked her whip changing it into a spear, she thrust the spear towards Ares but before she could follow through a lightning bolt struck the ground between the two.

"THAT'S ENOUGH! The child has been born it a boy, his name is Foréas Tis Santulan." Zeus announced.

"Of course father. I figured Kronos would speed up the pregnancy but did he even wait to find out if she was pregnant?" Athena asked, with an eyebrow raised.

"He had Hera on stand-by to tell him immediately. So, son, I'd hate to push more of my problems on you but will you be raising the child or not? Keep in mind if you refuse, should the Divine Devil set foot on the mountain again you will be our first line of defense. Just based on how quickly Athena just dealt with you that wouldn't go too well, and if what Hermes told me earlier is correct he didn't even touch you last time. So, what'll it be, Ares?" Zeus asked, tilting his head up.

"When he can walk and speak I will start training the boy, until then Athena can handle it she's better suited to indoctrination anyway," Ares said, as he turned to walk away.

"That's only because you're so simple-minded," Athena remarked, hitting a button on the inside of her shield returning to a gauntlet.

"If you have a problem with that father you can reconsider your decision to put the child in our care, you left it up to us and this is how we've chosen to do it." Ares declared before he leap across Mt.Olympus.

"So be it," Zeus said, he left before returning with the baby moments later the whole right side of the boy was blue.

Three years had passed and Foréas was on the ground doing push-ups over a carpet of flames high enough to scorch him if he's down for too long. Ares continued pacing around him counting each one as the toddler went up. After 500 Ares turned off the flames and Foréas almost collapsed but Ares put his foot under his chin. Ares materialized a hammer-like Mjolnir once again and used his foot to stand Foréas up.

"Not sleeping yet! You've still got 1000 hammer throws." Ares barked, as the child coughed up blood.

"Ares that's enough he's a toddler!" Athena demanded as she walked up behind him.

"Be quiet you had your three days, I'm only on the first of mine, he's still conscious he can keep going." Ares snapped back, throwing the hammer at Foréas' feet.

"It hurts Ares. Please let me rest, I beg of you." Foréas pleaded, hunched over arms limp and vigorously panting.

"You're in pain because of the Divine Devil, that monster is the reason you have to live like this. I'll make you a deal if you can strike me we'll call it early today, and starting tomorrow we'll skip right to sparring in your training." Ares said crushing the head of the hammer with his foot.

"How long do I have?" Foréas asked.

"Until you faint, starting now!" Ares declared. Foréas charged Ares with a right hook which he caught, Foréas then threw a left roundhouse Ares blocked it on his forearm, followed by a left hook which Ares also caught. Angered Foréas threw a right knee which was blocked creating an air vacuum on the other side of Ares's arm.

"STOP BLOCKING MY ATTACKS!" Foréas shrieked, reeling back, and launched a wicked headbutt that Ares just dodged throwing Foréas back over his head sending him 30 feet back. Fuming Foréas regained his footing before letting out a wail that could be heard across the mountain, his chest and biceps began to steam then quickly expanded and contracted. The ground around Foréas began to give, Ares blinked and Foréas was in his face. Surprised, he glanced down to see his feet driven into small craters into the ground. Ares panicked, a blade sprung from his chest, impaling Foréas but more angered than anything he rocked Ares with a massive headbutt simultaneously knocking him away and ripping the blade out of his torso. Foréas put his hand over his mouth as his cheeks puffed up, he looked to the side spitting out a puddle of blood onto the ground. He turned around and began to limp and stumble away as the wound steamed and slowly began to heal itself.

"Where are you going?" Athena shouted.

"To take a bath and sleep, I've got a long day of sparring tomorrow," Foréas yelled back.

"You should eat!" Athena responded.

"I'll get something from Auntie Aphrodite!" Foréas exclaimed, walking off into the distance.

"WHAT WAS THAT!? YOU COULD HAVE KILLED HIM." Athena screamed, scolding Ares.

"I'm surprised I didn't. I couldn't move so my body just acted on its own and I flared my power. Thanks to that though we discovered a major secret about Foréas. Of course, I'm not going to behead the boy but I would like to see how far his regeneration can go." Ares said, stroking his beard.

"YOU PUT A HOLE IN HIM!" Athena roared.

"AND IT'S GONE! SO SHUT UP!" Ares exclaimed.

"THE CHILD IS NOT A WEAPON TO BE SHARPENED, BROKEN, AND REPAIRED!" Athena howled, trembling in rage.

"He's whatever I say he is for the next two days," Ares responded, as he began to walk past Athena.

"YOU IGNORANT BRUTE!" Athena exclaimed.

"The Divine Devil feels nothing for the gods, if it weren't for me being an ignorant brute we'd probably be dead already," Ares said, walking away.

The next morning Foréas woke up, got dressed, and returned to the training grounds where Mjolnir and Thor's gauntlets were waiting for him. He slid the gauntlets on and they fit him like shirt sleeves, Foréas began placing the gauntlets up.

"That's not necessary boy, just take one of the laces in your teeth and the other in your opposite hand and pull as hard as you can," Ares instructed, walking up behind the boy. Foréas did as told and the gauntlet laced itself up and fitted to Foréas' much smaller frame and the process repeated with the other gauntlet. Ares put his hands together and materialized an English broadsword with a striking resemblance to Ascalon. Foréas hoisted up Mjolnir and a lightning bolt struck the head, turning and throwing it at Ares. Thinking quickly Ares outstretched the flat of the blade hoping to deflect the incoming hammer, but the hammer busted right through the blade. Ares bridged to dodge Mjolnir, Foréas was right there to step on Ares' face. Foréas was trying to stomp Ares' head into the ground but it wouldn't budge, Ares grabbed Foréas' ankle spinning around and whipping him into the ground. Foréas sprang back up jumping on Ares' back, opening his hand to call Mjolnir from behind Ares. Ares tried to bridge again but was too slow, Mjolnir grated the skin of his face cleaned off. Foréas sprang up off his back catching Mjolnir, he rushed at Ares once again but stopped dead as a blade sprang from Ares's chest.

"I don't think we should spar with weapons anymore Ares," Foréas said, tossing Mjolinir up in the air spinning it and catching it. Ares grits his teeth and bent down forward clutching his face.

"AHHHHHHHHHHHGH! Asclepius GET OVER HERE!" Ares howled, creating a magic circle in his hand, throwing it at the ground like a Frisbee. The circle bounced off the ground, making a portal mere feet from Ares. A surprisingly old-looking god bald, long thin withered gray beard, absurdly wrinkled skin, circles around his eyes so dark that all you can see is the light reflecting off of his pupils stepped through the portal with a cane.

"Dammit, Ares! This is the eighth time this month, and four of them were you trying to lift that damn hammer." Asclepius growled, smacking Ares upside his head with his cane. Ares's head was encompassed by a green sphere and his face was healed.

"Enough complaining already, you're lucky to be a god, to begin with," Ares responded, waving Asclepius off. Scoffing, Asclepius walks off back through the portal. As soon as the portal closed Ares turned to Foréas.

"So, are we going to keep going?" Foréas asked, pointing the head of Mjolnir at Ares.

"No, I believe you were right, we shouldn't keep sparring with weapons. Mjolnir just nicked me and I almost lost my head. I have the perfect partner in mind for you, but from now on we will only be sparing hand to hand." Ares said, lightly pushing Mjlonir away.

"So who's the partner?" Foréas asked, with a skeptic eyebrow raised.

"I'll introduce you on your free day so you can spend time together. If you two just start fighting without knowing each other all you'll know is conflict." Ares explained, leaving Foréas jaw a gape and he leaped backward. Foréas was above Ares targeting him with a dive kick, Ares grabbed Foréas' ankle bashing him into the ground and kicking him away. Ares chased him, dribbling him like a basketball. Foréas went limp and Ares hit him with a massive roundhouse causing him to spin away like a pinwheel in a hurricane. Ares began to scratch the back of his head with a concerned expression, but without Ares realizing it Foréas changed direction in midair. Foréas came back around the landing and earthshattering knee square on Ares' temple, his head whipped to the left and back causing it to vibrate. Ares fell backward out cold. With help from Ares' thick skull, Foréas managed to stop himself, shaking his head and stumbling as he walked away. Foréas made it a mile across the mountain before he was stopped by Athena.

"Foréas why aren't you training with Ares?" Athena asked, concerned as she grabbed his wrist

"I knocked him unconscious, so I figured we were done," Foréas responded, worried that he did something wrong. Athena released his wrist and stepped back in fear, she quickly shook her head coming to her senses.

"Foréas I want you to strike me in the head as hard you can." Athena declared, deeply exhaling and preparing herself.

"I'm sorry Athena I can't hit a girl that's not right," Foréas said, confused.

"I'm telling you to, so its fine, there's also going to come a time where you'll have to fight Harmonia and you must be willing to defend yourself. If you do it next week I'll let you have one of your days with me as a free day." Athena offered, Foréas' pupils dilated. The instant Athena finished talking, Foréas landed a massive knee to Athena's jaw. Athena blinked twice, slowly pushing down Foréas' knee.

"HOW?! You're completely unharmed!" Foréas exclaimed.

"Of course I am, I'm over a dozen times stronger than you, and Ares should be as well. Tell me what happened in that sparing match. Now." Athena ordered, annoyed right nostril flaring. Foréas explained exactly what happened during the match and was dismissed by Athena. Athena stormed over to Ares and lifted him by the collar, slapping him so loud it shook the mountain before dropping him onto his feet.

"Ahhhhh! WHAT NOW WOMAN?!" Ares barked, clutching the handprint on his face.

"You lost to the toddler you were supposed to be training!" Athena exclaimed, seething walls of Greek text appearing behind Athena over a thousand feet in the air.

"That's not possible," Ares responded, looking off wide-eyed into the distance.

"It happened, you used the child as a weapon to knock yourself out and all Hermes is gonna say is that you lost to the three-year-old Balance Bringer," Athena said, with a tiny smirk. Ares looked up behind Athena and the text reads 'God of War loses to toddler' over and over. Blades erupted from all over Ares's body. Athena turned and began to pant slowly but kept her grin as the text followed. Foréas wandered into a heavily forested area of the mountain and kept walking till he reached a clearing, hiding behind a bush at the sight of another person. He was a massive man, likely over ten feet tall with short dark-brown curly hair and matching beard, built as if chiseled out of marble, wearing a white toga with a golden belt, and surrounded by cattle.

"You can come out, I assure you I'm a gentle giant. Well as long as you're not Hera." Welcome????, slowly turning his head to the shrubbery Foréas was hiding in. Foréas slowly made his way over to the mountain of a man letting off a warm glow.

"Hello, sir," Foréas said, sheepishly still about ten feet away.

"Call me Heracles, little one. What's your name?" Heracles asked, extending his hand.

"I'm Foréas," Foréas responded, walking up closer and shaking Heracles' hand.

"Well Foréas, can you fly yet?" Heracles asked, with an excited smile.

"No," Foréas responded, looking at the ground in disappointment.

"I have a surprise for you." Heracles put his fingers between his lips whistling loudly.

"What are you?" Foréas asked, looking in the direction he whistled.

"Shhh. Give it a moment." Heracles responded before a cyclone began to approach them in the distance.

"Should we move?" Foréas asked, ready to step back.

"No, we'll be fine, don't worry about it," Heracles said, as the cyclone approached the clearing and dissipated. A gust of wind ripped through the clearing and a winged horse had appeared before them.

"What is this?!" Foréas exclaimed, starry-eyed stepping up to the horse.

"This is Pegasus, take it easy on him pal it's his first flight," Heracles said, petting Pegasus' mane before putting Foréas on his back and tapping the winged horse twice. Pegasus began slowly flapping his wings and the two had taken to the skies. Once they'd made it past the Forrest Pegasus' speed doubled, Foréas watched in awe as the scenery below them became a blur. Pegasus moving at sonic speeds had reached the edge of the mountain and abruptly dipped as Foréas continued giggling in jubilation. The two blew through a dark place passing over five ever-winding rivers and Foréas tucked his face into Pegasus' mane. Pegasus flew for about another five minutes before coming across a large beautiful wheat field below a gorgeous blue sky. Pegasus seemed to stop mid-air along with everything else. Kronos put his hand on Foréas' head from behind.

"Who are you?" Foréas asked, looking around as everything stood still.

"I wasn't entirely sure at first but now I know I'm your father, Kronos. I'm also the Titan with domain over time, I was perfectly content with staying out of your life but since you came to me I'll leave the choice up to you. Those two give you a free day right, well you can come here and spend time with me if you desire. I'll let you get back to Heracles now though." Kronos said, descending to the ground and returning the flow of time in the area to normal. Pegasus kept flying as if nothing happened, returning to Heracles.

"That was amazing! Everything below was just a blur. We made it around the whole mountain." Foréas exclaimed, elated as he jumped off Pegasus' back.

"I'm glad you enjoyed it, you can go for a flight whenever you want. Just come see me and I'll call Pegasus." Heracles said, patting the grass signaling Foréas to sit down. Foréas sat down and the two spoke and laughed together till the sunset.

The next morning came and Foréas arrived at the sparring grounds. Ares smashed into the ground creating a three-mile crater around the two. Ares' eyes were bloodshot and he was sheathing blade tips kept popping out and retracting back into his skin.

"Today is a special sparring session Foréas, we're going to test the limits of your regeneration," Ares said, enthusiastically panting as his right eye twitched. Foréas opened his mouth to speak, but before he could get any words out his jaw was gone and his mouth was spraying blood. Ares' right fist had crossed Foréas' face, wrapping his hand around the tiny forearm of Foréas Ares whipped him through the air, tearing his broken arm from his body sending him flying away. Before Foréas could go far Ares was already behind him, knocking him to the ground, bouncing him off of the crater and back down. Clouds of steam surrounded Foréas as Ares slowly descended, having let off some steam of his own. Ares gradually made his way over to what is now a plume of mist, he stopped as he saw a dim red glow. On the other side of the steam, Foréas' injuries were slowly healing themselves as a scarlet light peaked through the cracking surface of his right eye. Foréas' hair rose and began to wave as the scarlet light burst through his right eye and corrupted the steam, Ares jumped back and put his arms up. The scarlet light was almost as blinding as the sun itself and it was mere inches from Ares' face, Foréas had shot out from the steam. Ares watched in amazement as wounds that would've taken minutes to stop bleeding were completely restored. A forearm and hand shot out from Foréas' stub of an arm as he wound up swiping at

Ares's head knocking him back sixty feet. Foréas' jaw regenerated in the midst of him letting out a thunderous bloodcurdling shriek, he charged towards the God of War and Ares looked up Foréas was biting at his throat. A blade quickly protruded from his adam's apple, stopping Foréas dead and impaling him through his mouth. Foréas slapped down through the blade as Ares grabbed his face, forcing him to the ground and keeping Foréas there with a knee across the rest of his body. "Athena! Come here now!" Ares demanded, Foréas flailing around causing the mountain to rumble. A magic circle appeared in front of Ares and Athena.

"What did you do to him?!" Athena asked, panicking as she knelt to look at Foréas.

"That's not important right now, just examine him while I can still hold him. He's getting too unpredictable to deal with." Ares grunted, amidst Foréas rabidly jerking around. Athena put a hand on Foréas and a magic circle quickly scanned him up and down, she stood back up and a book materialized in her other hand. She opened the book and began flipping through the pages. Athena's eyebrows raised as she closed the book with a thud and it disappeared as a magic circle scanned over it.

"Hermes, I require your assistance," Athena called out, moments later a streak of feathers blew past her.

"At your service, Lady Athena," Hermes said, lowering his head to Athena.

"A little busy for formalities," Ares said, tempering his grip not to crush Foréas' skull.

"Yes that's right, you've been following the boy. Has he made any close companions?" Athena asked.

"Yes. Only just yesterday though, it's Zeus' favorite demigod child." Hermes responded.

"Ares quick, off the boy!" Athena commanded, as she turned around and extended her hand making a magic circle under the two. Ares jumped off of Foréas pushing him through the portal created from the circle. Foréas landed in the clearing yesterday, Heracles glanced up to see Foréas lunging toward him jaw agape. Heracles flicked him in the forehead sending

Foréas yards back, he stood up and began walking to Foréas. Foréas sprang towards Heracles, biting his neck but his teeth just barely broke the skin. Heracles wrapped his arms around Foréas squeezed until there was a pop and Foréas slumped over Heracles arm. Heracles dropped Foréas and turned around as his eyes began to water, he heard movement in the grass and turned around to see Foréas gone. Foréas dropped down from the sky but was stopped by a massive hand across his head.

"Foréas, look at me. Listen to my voice. I don't want to hurt you anymore. I don't like hurting anyone. Snap out of it please!" Heracles begged, putting his hand over Foréas' right eye and starring into his left. Foréas' hair slowly began to fall and the red light that peaked through Heracles' fingers began to dim. Heracles pulled Foréas in for a much less lethal hug this time, Foréas fell unconscious and Heracles scooped him up. A vacuum was created by how fast Heracles flew over to the sparring ground.

"He did it!" Ares exclaimed, as his excitement turned to fear when he saw the agitated disappointment on Heracle's face. Heracles descended to the ground and put Foréas in Athena's arms.

"Nothing you two do could surprise me at this point, but HOW COULD YOU BRING A CHILD INTO WHATEVER THIS IS?" Heracles snapped, before letting out a deep breath through his nose. Athena quickly explained the situation with Tobias to Heracles.

"So you see Foréas is our only true chance against the Divine Devil," Athena said, Foréas stirring in her arms.

"I'll handle it." Heracles declared, turning to Hermes and giving a nod.

"Of course Heracles, as you wish," Hermes said, as the wings on his boots began to flap rapidly and he took off. Hermes flew forward, disappearing and reappearing in the Ashes of Asgard.

"Hermes!" Harmonia exclaimed, before getting sent flying by a roundhouse from Tobias. Tobias' eyebrows raised as he turned to look at Hermes.

"As the mortals would say, who wants the smoke?" Tobias asked, an arrogant grin lacing his face. He closed his eyes for a moment, activating the All-Seeing Eye for a birds-eye view of his surroundings to casually dodge an incoming attack from Harmonia.

"Heracles," Hermes said, jumping back when Tobias drew Ascalon.

"Dimension Cutter!" Tobias exclaimed, slashing downward and extending his hand back to Harmonia. Harmonia took his hand and the two flew through the portal.

"What weapon would you like Heracles?" Ares asked, putting his hands together.

"An impractically large and sharp ax," Heracles responded, looking over his shoulder as a hole in the air was seemingly cut by nothing. Tobias flew through with Harmonia.

"Please tell me you've gotten stronger from the last time Harmonia would have met you," Tobias called out, arrogantly. Heracles did a double-take, appalled at the unyielding and insulting arrogance of the Divine Devil.

"Can't say I have, but going off of what I heard this won't take long regardless." Heracles shot back, grabbing the comically large ax Ares created for him.

"I'm just gonna warn you, Harmonia and I are a good bit stronger than Thor was," Tobias said, his smile not budging. Ares fell to his knees and Athena's heart dropped.

"YOU'RE BLUFFING!" Heracles barked, causing Foréas to start waking up.

"This would be a lot more fun if I was. We've done nothing but fight for the past three years, well almost nothing but fight." Tobias said, winking at Ares. Athena jumped back 300 yards with Foréas putting him on the ground.

"Foréas, the one before Heracles. That is the Divine Devil, watch closely how he fights." Athena said, pointing at Tobias. Heracles charged Tobias swinging the ax overhead and Tobias just stood there, taking the blow. The ax just bounced off Tobias' skull, the head cracked and fell apart as Heracles was bounced back slightly from the recoil. Harmonia snickered and Tobias broke right out into laughter, Heracles regained his composure but was being blown back tens of feet by Tobias' every laugh.

"Oh, WHAT THE FUCK!" Heracles exclaimed, planting his feet and putting his arms up before rushing at Tobias. He reached the Divine Devil and took a swing, he just ate it and swung back. Tobias tried to stop himself from following through but it was too late, Heracles' head spun all the way around and flew off landing mere inches from Foréas. Foréas dropped to his knees covering his mouth with his hands, Ares tapped Heracles head to the side with his foot before Foréas threw up on the ground and began trembling.

"Guess he couldn't…go the distance," Tobias said, with a shit-eating grin.

"So are we done here?" Harmonia asked, rolling her eyes so hard her irises almost continued off of her face.

"Not quite, that was way too fast I want at least one more fight," Tobias said, closing his eyes before his forehead lit up momentarily. "Dimension Cutter." He called out, as the others except for Harmonia only saw a portal open and he sheathes his sword.

"Elysium!" Athena exclaimed. Foréas looked up and terror struck his face.

"We have to stop him! He's going to kill my father!" Foréas cried, tears streaming down his face. Harmonia followed Tobias through the portal and it closed behind them.

"Unfortunately if anyone could even think of stopping him right now it would be your father. Watch the fight closely." Athena said, as she put her palm out in front of Foréas, a magic circle appeared above her hand and they could now see what was happening in Elysium. Tobias descended upon Kronos.

"You, we're fighting right now. This isn't a request, defend yourself or die." Tobias said, drawing Ascalon and pointing it at Kronos. Kronos sighed, standing up annoyed.

"Well if you insist," Kronos responded. The two then charged at one another, Kronos then kicked Ascalon out of his hand sending it flying like a dart into Harmonia. She quickly dodged the blade and leap back away from the fight.

Trying to follow through he couldn't move his leg, turned to the side Kronos began turning his face forward pushing Tobias' knee back in the process.

"Guess I took it a bit too easy on you after accidentally killing Heracles," Tobias said, satisfied. Their eyes then met, that instant Tobias lept back and quickly got behind Kronos and closed his eyes.

"Harmonia, I'm using the All-Seeing to communicate with you telepathically. I need you to do me a favor," Tobias thought to Harmonia.

"Anything, what is it?" Harmonia responded. "Throw Ascalon not to me anywhere just make sure it stays out of his line of sight,"

"Alright" Harmonia replied moments before throwing Ascalon. Tobias charged at Kronos. Seconds before Tobias was about to connect he made eye contact once more he saw clocks appear in each of Kronos' eyes. Tobias threw a kick to the ribs but Kronos didn't even react. Behind Kronos, Tobias had seen had moved from where it was before he'd thrown the kick.

"As I thought," Tobias exclaimed.

"He found out," Kronos growled, gritting his teeth.

"You can only stop what you can see," Tobias responded.

"What of it, you can't do anything with that information." Kronos barked, clearly shaken up.

"Simple if you can't see me you can't stop me."

"Wait what you mean by that... he's gone!" Kronos screamed, rapidly glancing around.

"As I said before if you can't see me you can't stop, but the problem with going this fast is staying under the speed of light if I were to go too much faster everything just turns black. I hope you can hear what I'm saying. I've never tested this before so I don't know," Tobias' voice echoed moments after small craters started appearing on Kronos' body. He then started letting out agonizing roars of pain.

"How are you moving so fast without bending or tearing the space around you?" Kronos asked, panting and down to a knee.

"It's not that complex, you know how gods have their source of power and it has to be transferred through physical contact but since the power source itself is intangible I can wrap it around my body and have it not affect space-time in any way," Tobias explained, before stopping behind him. Tobias then ran up to Kronos' back and stomped his head into the ground three times with his foot still on Kronos' head he spun around on it grinding it in. Tobias followed it up with a massive punt to the skull and face of Kronos propelling him into the air he then charged at him with a steady barrage of punches, kicks, elbows, and knees.

"This is over, with the eradication of the Norse Pantheon, the fall of the most powerful of the Egyptian gods, and the defeat of the Titan with domain over time you can send the rest of the Greek Pantheon my disappointment it's officially no one can stop me the only bones I left unbroken are the ones in your mouth so you can tell the story of what took place here," Tobias said, with equal parts disappointment in his voice. He cut back into Mount Olympus with Kronos still by the neck with Ascalon in hand, Tobias laughed in Ares' face. Tobias began carving something into the training ground with Kronos' face and left his mark, being an upside-down cross attached to a right-side-up below it with a backward capital d on the left side of the upside-down cross and a normal capital d on the right side of the right-side-up cross. Tobias then threw Kronos to the side like a piece of garbage.

"Tobias, you've proven your point, let's go home," Harmonia said, agitation building in her voice.

"Fine, I've had my fun. Goodbye, dearest father-in-law. Dimension Cutter." Tobias called out, slashing down into the Ashes of Asgard and the pair left. Foréas sat there, trembling, rocking back and forth, tears streaming down his face.

"Foréas calm down, Heracles will be fine and so will your father. This is why we need you, if the Divine Devil keeps getting stronger at this rate you're going to be the only one strong enough to stop him." Ares said, extending his hand out to the side and a similar magic circle appeared over his palm and expanded. A portal opened and Asclepius walked through picking Heracles head up by the hair. He took the head over to Heracles body, putting it right above the neck. A needle of white light appeared on the tip of Asclepius's index finger, his hand became a blur as he stitched the head back to the body of Heracles and the seam slowly faded away. Asclepius' eyes began to glow, could see an x-ray of Heracle's body but then it went deeper. There was a dim light throughout Heracles' entire body except where the heart would be and then Asclepius looked a bit deeper as his eyes grew brighter, there was a space just smaller than Heracles heart. Light surrounded each of Asclepius' fingers and he jabbed his hand into Heracles' chest but there was no blood. Meanwhile, on a plane of existence, no one can see a portal began to open above the sky of Mount Olympus and an orange orb began floating towards it. Asclepius cut into the space so some of the light from Heracles body could pool into it, he pulled on the light and threw some of the light into the sky as if it were a rope. A green aura stretched from the other side of the portal and latched on to the rope before it could reach the orb, ripping a green orb down to Heracles' body. Moments later Heracles' body floated up off the ground slightly and seemingly vanished. Heracles reappeared on the other side of the mountain struggling to stop flying.

"What's this? I have so much...power." Heracles breathed, with a maddened chuckle.

"I'm sure it was just a startling experience for Heracles, let's just give him a while to gather," Athena said, hiding her suspicion as she caressed the back of Foréas' head.

"Get some rest, tomorrow I'll be introducing you to your new weapons sparring partner," Ares said, whilst Asclepius was healing Kronos.

"No," Foréas said, too tired to shake anymore.

"What?" Ares barked, through gritted teeth with a flared nostril.

"Tomorrow is my free day and I'm going to spend it with Aunt Aphrodite," Foréas responded, falling asleep on Athena.

CHAPTER 10

The Balance Bringer

It's been 7 years in the Realm Of The Gods and Tobias was just about to return to Heaven with Harmonia now with a slight baby bump.

"Hey I'm ba…," Tobias was interrupted by a flying hammer approaching his face, and sliced the hammer in half with Ascalon.

"Tobias I was born to beat you, my name is Foréas Tis Santulan. You can just call me Foréas," Foréas declared.

"How the Hell did that hammer survive?!" Tobias questioned.

"This hammer is more durable than you can imagine." Foréas responded, seeing the head of Mjolnir crumble before eyes and feeling the air hit his wrists.

"You can't even hold it without these, pathetic." Tobias said, disappointed as he spun the laces of the gauntlets around his finger.

"You couldn't have, HOW?! I didn't even see you move." Foréas exclaimed, his hands trembling in fear.

"You never stood a chance, assuming you're about as strong as I was last I went to Mt. Olympus which is the last time anyone but Harmonia would've seen me. I'm more than ten times stronger than I was back then. I finally understand Thor's warning, he wasn't being arrogant. I'm so much more powerful now that if I were to just twitch while in contact with you the transfer of power would be enough to erase you from existence. No level of restraint could keep that from happening. So to make this more interesting and demonstrate the difference in our power I'll only use a tenth of my blade to kill you. Death by a million paper-cuts as the mortals would say." Tobias explained, retracting Ascalon and throwing it at Foréas leaving a fine scratch on his face. To Foréas Tobias had vanished but to Harmonia he was like a cat chasing around a yarn ball, scraping Foréas with the compacted Ascalon. Tobias left Foréas a fine bloody pulp within the span of a second.

"Was that really necessary?" Harmonia asked, snatching Ascalon from mid-air and handing it to Tobias.

"Hey, he came here to kill me. I merely defended myself, I hope Zeus thinks of a stronger pair of parents next time and has their 'champion' train for a lot longer." Tobias said, expanding Ascalon and sheathing it as he began walking towards the gates. God heard a boom from the other side of Heaven before Tobias and Harmonia were standing at his throne.

"Tobias, what brings you back?" God asked, trembling.

"Harmonia is pregnant as you can see and my father turned this into a place where no pain could be felt, we'll talk about that later. But for now, get up." Tobias commanded, rubbing Harmonia's stomach and snickering as he could practically see God's heart drop.

"You have a lot of trust in us, Tobias." God said, standing up and stepping aside.

"Oh it has nothing to do with trust. Show him Harmonia, if you would?" Tobias asked. Harmonia sat down on the throne and began to twirl her finger as short threads of light spun around it like a pinwheel before stiffening her finger, instantly casting the threads into the heads of every angel in Heaven. She quickly withdrew every thread but the one attached to Azrael, holding her forehead.

"Jesus, go heal the Balance Bringer." God's words echoed in Jesus' mind.

"Yes father, I'll be right over there." Jesus responded, rushing through where the gates used to be and stopping at the sight of a beating heart with branching veins, arteries, and blood vessels. Jesus put his hands out and a faint green glow surrounded the regenerating body of Foréas, in mere seconds a brain formed from the blood vessels, the spine and the skeletal system, the nervous system, the muscular system, and finally the half blue skin. Foréas quickly sat up panting wildly, crushing Jesus' head in the process and rapidly looking around. Jesus regenerated and cleared his throat as Foréas stood up, raising his right hand.

"What? Are you expecting thanks? Your thanks you is me allowing everyone in this kingdom to live, seeing as you're harboring the Divine Devil." Foréas said, turning his back to Jesus as Mjolnir flew into his hand. Mjolnir shrank down to the size of a bottle opener and Foréas put it on like a necklace, he raised his left hand palm-up creating a magic circle. As Foréas floated up through the portal and appeared on the other side before a man around the same height as Tobias, but he was a hero, almost literally chiseled out of marble. The man was clad in lustrous and reflective silver armor, clean shaven and with shoulder-length curly brown hair.

"So is the Divine Devil dead?" The man asked, already fully aware of the answer.

"No Achilles he's not." Foréas responded, reluctantly, gripping the miniature Mjolnir hanging around his neck.

"How many times have I told you to make sure you knew your enemy before fighting them!" Achilles told Foréas, getting in his face. Foréas looked to the ground ashamed.

"Well now I don't have to learn anything because the fool told me exactly how strong he was himself, so follow me we're going to the Mortal Realm. I'll be back to kill the Divine Devil before he realizes I lived. Selecting you for my sparring partner was the smartest decision Ares has ever made." Foréas said, dispersing the circle below him and creating a larger one above the both of them. He shot up through it grabbing Achilles by the hair on the way up, the two appeared in the outer reaches of space. The two separate and collide literally head to head knocking each other backwards, sending shockwaves throughout space shaking the stars in the distance. Blood trickled down Foréas' cracked forehead before freezing up and crumbling away as the wound healed. Foréas appeared above Achilles throwing a huge axe kick just to be blocked, continuing his momentum into an axe handle and sending Achilles rolling before kicking him away. Achilles stopped himself in time for Foréas to show up in front him, he punched clean through Foréas' gut, he grimaced before kneeing Achilles in the chest launching far above. Foréas cut Achilles off and knocked him into a remote planet, Foréas went head first into Achilles sending the pair into the planet's core creating a massive explosion.

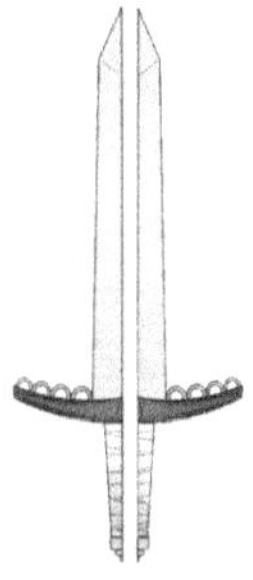

CHAPTER 11

Weapons for the Future

As Tobias spun Thor's gauntlets around his finger he looked to the sheathed Ascalon on his hip. He then looked off into the distance caressing Harmonia's stomach.

"Harmonia, what if the other gods smarten up and send more than one hybrid for me next time and they're capable? We're powerful but neither of us can be in two places at once. Eventually, they'll find out about and target the child." Tobias said, worry in his voice.

"Children," God said, as a chill ran up his spine.

"What?" Tobias and Harmonia both responded, looking to God.

"There are two souls in her womb, you're having twins," God responded, squeezing his fist reluctantly.

"I have to go!" Tobias exclaimed, flying through the portal as Ascalon slid back into the scabbard. He arrived in the Ashes of Asgard, using the All-Seeing to gather information on Mjolnir. "Dimension Cutter," Tobias called out, going through another portal. He floated above a massive mountain, easily half the size of Earth. Ascalon became a blur before Tobias sheathed it again and as if he'd blown out a birthday candle, half a mountain formed from the dust of the mountain below Tobias. Tobias compacted Ascalon, focusing on the rain guard before a magic circle spun around it for a moment and then faded away. He dropped Ascalon into the hole, the circle around the compacted Ascalon lit up and Tobias appeared right next to the dagger.

"Brokkr, do you know this one?" A short and stout man asked his brother behind him.

"No Sindri, but that blade is Ascalon and it has more than ten times the amount of power flowing through it than Thor had in his entire body. Plus his body emanates with the ghost of Runic Magic." Brokkr responded, trembling as electricity sparked around the glowing lens above his right eye.

"Oh there are those who don't know who I am, then again I guess I did kill everyone who could've told you. I accidentally burned down Asgard so all the gods are dead, I also burned the branch that connected Asgard to Yggdrasil which inadvertently severed the entire dimension's link to Runic Magic. I am Tobias, known primarily to the other gods as the Divine Devil. You just reassured me that you two are Brokkr and Sindri, you're going to forge me two weapons, and this should be all you need. Dimension Cutter." Tobias said, cutting open a portal and ripping two bars off of the gates of heaven. He plucked a hair from his head and shaved off a tiny piece of Ascalon before laying them together, making a thread. Tobias walked over and set the materials aside on the table.

"Are there any specific weapons you want to be made or do you want us to see what we can do with what you gave us?" Brokkr asked, watching the power fade from the hair follicle.

"Oh, yeah. I guess that would help. A long sword that converts into bladed t   onfa. Also, Gauntlets that after every 5 years of wearing them the wearer's strength gets cut in half, I would like one of the Gauntlets to be cable of shooting arrows as strong as the wearer and the other to convert into a shield that repels all things on contact with the same amount of force created when one hundred atoms are split. For convenience have them turn into bracelets, and don't forget a scabbard for the sword. Dimension Cutter." Tobias said, returning to the Ashes of Asgard.

"They'll be done in 4 months!" Sindri called out from the other side of the portal as it closed. Harmonia appeared behind Tobias, wrapping her arms around him and running her hand down his chest while breathing deeply up the back of his neck.

"I don't know who you are, but you aren't Harmonia. Your heartbeat makes my stomach turn," Tobias growled, as his irises burst into golden rings of fire. He slipped out of Harmonia's embrace, the instant he saw her the golden light began to fade in and out from his eyes. Tobias hunched down grasping his head. "What's happening? You're not Harmonia, I know you aren't, she's pregnant with my children but my body won't let me hurt you." Tobias grunted, one hand holding his head the other shaking above the handle of Ascalon.

"Your heart pounds like the rhythm of a war drum, stirring conflict with every beat. It's irresistible in more ways than one." Harmonia swooned, blushing as she floated up through a magic circle.

"Dimension Cutter!" Tobias gasped, gathering himself as he flew through.

"I went there to fight him and got scared, but the mind of the Divine Devil is far more fragile than I could've hoped for," Harmonia said, as luminescent green ashes crumbling from her body are carried away by the wind revealing Heracles.

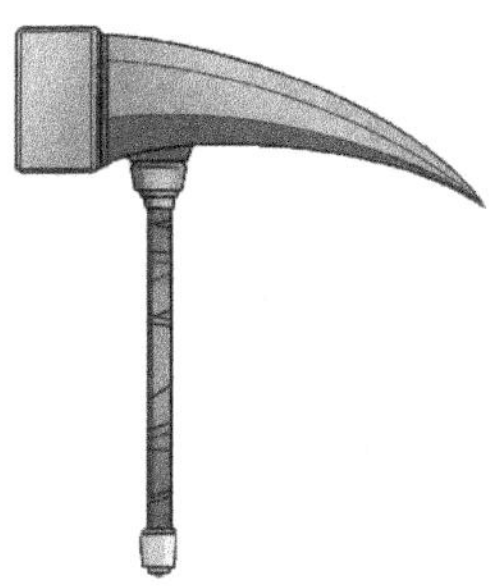

CHAPTER 12

Round 2

....

Tobias' children will be born in another four months, he in his confusion and frustration with himself spends two months in the Realm of The Gods sitting in Hell as a way of banging his head against the proverbial wall. That's an incredible feat considering in Hell time passes as it would in the Mortal Realm and as a result of what happened in the burning of Asgard Tobias is forced to bathe in his gilded flames. When the distracted Divine Devil opened the portal something slithered out. Spending the first two weeks screaming in agony, he then went silent the rest of his time in Hell. Coming out blood-red Tobias would then be drenched in Holy Water. Tobias then flew through the far end of the known universe in days cutting through stars like a hot knife through butter until the biggest star, Betelgeuse, slipped a grape in between his teeth.

"Ascalon Flame," Tobias said, as the blade was consumed by gilded flames. He sliced the star clean in half and one of the halves was erased from existence, the star's core immediately collapsed in on itself forming a black hole. Tobias could've distorted space-time with the power he used to cut that star. He swung Ascalon with all his might at the dark hole the two forces stalled out and nothing happened. Tobias cut his finger on Ascalon, he then with a taste went into bloodlust again he then made contact with the black hole but it didn't disappear he then gave it a tap. The resulting impact created another Big bang and by extension another universe. Tobias then bit down on the grape, turning off his bloodlust. He spent the remaining time exploring the fresh universe.

Meanwhile, Foréas is causing earthquakes on a remote large planet tossing and turning in his sleep. Now when he flexes his muscles it can cause shock waves that have enough force to push large constellations. Foréas has also been improving his mental prowess and has developed new abilities.

4 months have passed and Tobias was waiting in Heaven for Harmonia to go into labor. A lightning bolt struck in the vast star-less void, left by Tobias' show of force. Tobias had decided to let the mortals raise his children, leaving the choice of the family up to Jesus because to him it wouldn't matter. After witnessing the birth of his son and daughter, Leist and Chrysafén, Tobias returned to the universe he'd recently created. He arrived to see a planet the size of the Milky Way, with an acropolis that almost spans the planet's borders. With pillars as tall as the distance around the sun and as wide as Jupiter, it was an impossible marvel of Architecture. Tobias closed his eyes for a moment as he drew and compacted Ascalon, the magic circle on the rain guard reappeared as his forehead flashed. He threw Ascalon, Foréas pulled Mjolnir from his neck and returned it to its regular size. Foréas cocked back to return Ascalon to sender, but the dagger flew clean through the head of Mjolnir. Tobias appeared behind Foréas then pushed his face into the ground and dragged it for a while before throwing him off into the air.

"Oh you lived, HOW KIND OF YOU!" Tobias said, his voice cracking with a maddened giggle. Foréas stabilized holding out his left arm, Mjolnir was in his hand less than a second later. Foréas threw Mjolnir, Tobias dodged the hammer and the bolt that followed it but then another struck him square in the back but left no open wound.

"What are you? That should've impaled you with such heat and precision you didn't even bleed." Foréas exclaimed, looking down to see Tobias' hand at his neck.

"I am who you were born, raised, and trained to kill right? Yeah, fighting with Harmonia is fun, but there's just something euphoric about fighting with the intent to kill." Tobias said, the golden light in his irises flaring up. He wound up as far back as he could, splattering Foréas' head leaving only his jaw. Tobias repeated this four more times as Foréas regenerated.

"Will you STOP THAT? It's not fucking working!" Foréas yelled, growing more annoyed than afraid of him as Tobias did it one more time.

"You're right, maybe I am taking the wrong approach," Tobias responded, gouging out and crushing Foréas' heart. The hole in Foréas' chest closed and Tobias burned up the blood on his hand to rub his chin thinking as the rest flooded down his elbow. Tobias teleported himself and Foréas to Ascalon before snatching it up and expanding it.

"Ascalon Flame!" Tobias screamed, looking Foréas dead in the eyes winding back so it almost cut through him from the other side. He swung with as much force as possible like he was cracking a whip, slicing clean through and cauterizing Foréas' neck. Tobias watched in amazement as what should've been a scar started regenerating but slower and uglier than previously. Foréas' mouth had finished regenerating.

"You're dead!" Foréas growled, 15 seconds later the rest of his head had finished regenerating but his left eye was gone. A burst of scarlet light gushed from the empty socket as Foréas raised his right arm calling Mjolnir with a bolt of scarlet lightning. Foréas hit Tobias with Mjolnir making him spin, sending him rifling into one of the pillars. The right side of Tobias' head was caved in and he was bleeding from his eye.

"Ah what are these things made of? I guess I'm not the only one whose biology came with certain perks. Speaking of which, that's my blood. Let's see if he can keep up." Tobias said, spitting out a mouth of blood as the gold fades from irises and explodes from his pupils as the mirrored crosses. A crazed

Foréas rushed Tobias and the two butted heads, sending them apart and crushing Foréas' in the process. Tobias kicked Foréas square in the forehead and he began spinning but couldn't go anywhere because Tobias bounced him off the ground like a basketball. Tobias punched Foréas in the gut wrapping him around his fist, following it up with a knee to the chin launching him away. Tobias looked up into the distance watching him clear half the acropolis before intercepting him and knocking him to the ground with an axe handle.

"Why haven't I received any fatal damage from this onslaught? It hurt more than having my head destroyed. Why are you so arrogant I bashed your face in?" Foréas asked, writhing in pain.

"When my Bloodlust activates and my soul awakens I gain complete control over the flow of power throughout my body. I've been hitting you way harder, I just took every ounce of power out of my fists." Tobias explained, lifting Foréas by the collar.

"So you've been slapping me this whole time?" Foréas asked, clutching Tobias' wrist as his arm was erased from existence.

"Now you're getting it, you gave me a lot of fun but I have to end this now. I have responsibilities, being a parent and all." Tobias said, licking his chops.

"You'd have to mortally wound me at least 100,000 more times," Foréas responded, as his arms and legs continued to be erased with every strike thrown.

"If your body can keep up I can do it in less than a minute," Tobias said, throwing Foréas away like garbage. He cut Foréas off, clapping his head into mush. A shrieking sound is heard in the distance approaching Foréas and Tobias. Tobias side-stepped, grabbing Foréas by the head and holding him directly in the arrow's path. The arrow shot by Harmonia ripped Foréas' body from his head, pinning him to one of the far pillars like a thumbtack.

"How could a mere arrow have such power?" Foréas asked, trying to pull out the arrow as every muscle and vein in his body tensed up.

"Because it was fired by me," Harmonia said, flying up next to Tobias as their children watched in the distance. She planted one on the lips of the Divine Devil and the mirrored crosses reverted to his regular pupils, with a tight embrace the golden light faded from his irises as well.

"I guess we'll just have to put a 'to be continued on our final battle," Tobias said arrogantly, leaving with his wife and children.

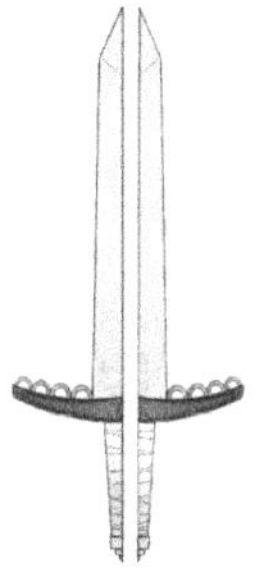

CHAPTER 13

Offspring beyond Comprehension

"Aren't you worried he's going to escape?" Leist asked, afraid.

"Why would I be, that arrow is as powerful as your mother and I, I doubt both us at the same time could remove it. Even if he did get out he's no threat to me and by the time I'm done he won't be a threat to you either." Tobias said, confidently as he slashed open a portal to the Ashes of Asgard.

"What about mother?" Chrysafén asked, fear traced Tobias' eyes for a moment while he followed his family through the portal.

"We'll talk about that later." Tobias responded, trying to sound as confident as earlier.

"Where are we?" Leist asked, looking into the lush expanse on the edge of a forest.

"This is the Ashes of Asgard." Tobias said, kneeling down to the ground.

"Ashes? This place is beautiful!" Chrysafén exclaimed, in awe.

"That's because of a special illusion created by your mother's magic." Tobias clarified, putting his hand on the ground as a massive magic circle appeared and began to crack.

"What are you doing?!" Harmonia asked, almost panicked as her magic circle shattered.

"Just cast it again." Tobias said, as the greenery dissolved into light and floated away.

"That took me three hours to cast before." Harmonia objected.

"Yes but you haven't been waking up hours earlier than me for ten years just to make breakfast, that's not the woman I married." Tobias said.

"I guess when you can access basically any information, it's hard to keep secrets from you." Harmonia said, throwing a magic circle like a discus. The circle flew hundreds of miles away before expanding to encompass all of the Ashes of Asgard, restoring the fona as it dropped.

"Leist, Chrysafén I want you two to fight each other without your weapons. The only rule is no killing. There is no surrender, I will decide when the fight is over and who wins." Tobias said, waiting for Harmonia's objection.

"Right now?" Chrysafén asked.

"Unless your mother has anything to say about it." Tobias answered.

"No, I'm as interested as you are to see how this plays out and figure out where we're going from here." Harmonia responded, walking back to grab something from the cabin.

"If you insist." Leist said, taking a deep breath.

"But father, I don't know how to take these gauntlets off." Chrysafén said, confused, pulling at the back of the shield.

"There should be hook shaped pins on the underside of them. Turn the pins and that should disarm the weapons." Tobias explained, as the shield and bow turned into gold bracelets over the gauntlets. Tobias gave the signal to start as Harmonia returned with a picnic basket and blanket. Chrysafén rushed Leist, throwing a punch that landed square in the gut. Leist grabbed Chrysafén's wrist, twisting her arm and punching through her elbow sending bones shooting through the other side. Tobias was about to get up but Harmonia put her hand on Tobias' shoulder.

"No other god or goddess would stop there, this was the whole point in having them fight in the first place. We can teach them to hold back later, for now we have to know how we're going to train them." Harmonia said, handing Tobias a sandwich. Leist immediately remorseful stepped back and was greeted with a knee to the forehead, followed by an axe kick to the cranium. Chrysafén ran over, gritting her teeth with tears in her eyes and punted Leist hundreds of feet away. Harmonia snapped her fingers and a magic circle showing Leist appeared in front of them. Chrysafén lifted Leist up by the collar and head-butted him in the face three times, Leist pulled back jacking Chrysafén's jaw, sending her back ten feet. Chrysafén spat out a mouth of blood, Tobias' breathed a sigh of relief as Chrysafén kneed Leist in the face, knocking him to the ground. A familiar red aura pulsed from Leist's body just before Tobias appeared at Chrysafén's side.

"Grab on, NOW! This fight is over." Tobias demanded, urgently as Chrysafén wrapped her right arm tightly around Tobias and the two shot thousands of miles into the sky. Harmonia had Leist by the collar and was pouring a thermos of soup in his mouth and the red aura faded.

"I know why it happened, but tell me what exactly happened." Harmonia asked, as Tobias descended with Chrysafén.

"Good to know that's hereditary. It's a defense mechanism I call Bloodlust, when I taste my blood my body floods my power to whatever threat I make contact with. If you know you're going to be ok when it activates you can decide what is and isn't a threat, but if you're unsure your body takes control and decides for you." Tobias explained, letting out a sigh.

"That's why you're always so certain you'll win, *you have to be*." Harmonia said, keeping that last part to herself.

"Asclepius get over here, our children need medical attention!" Tobias yelled, loud enough to be heard from any part of Mt.Olympus.

"Oh, don't worry as long as I'm in the same dimension I can open a door to his ward from anywhere." Harmonia said, flicking her wrist and creating a familiar magic circle. Asclepius walked through the magic circle, Cain in hand.

"How is he so old?" Tobias asked, confused as Asclepius made his way over to Chrysafén.

"Hades got tired of him brining mortals back from the dead so they granted him godhood to keep him out of the Mortal Realm." Harmonia explained, watching a faint green light encompass Chrysafén.

"Can you teach me how to do that, please." Chrysafén requested, quietly watching her wound close and her arm contort back into place.

"Of course I can but you won't learn overnight, with your potential I estimate it will take you about two weeks to learn the healing arts, with an extra month to learn anatomy and medicine." Asclepius replied.

"Father?" Chrysafén asked timidly.

"Sure go ahead, it'll be great for you." Tobias said, optimistically.

"Thank you," Chrysafén said, content.

"I think I'm going to hang around here for a month, I plan on making Athena my teacher." Leist said, brashly as Athena walked up behind him.

"Oh you want to learn from me? I'm humbled." Athena said, sarcastically, desperately trying to hide her fear of the Divine Devil.

"Is that a no? I couldn't tell under all your arrogance." Leist responded, turning to Athena with a grin on his face.

"I don't know if you have the patience to learn, or even the intelligence to make good use of my teachings." Athena said, taunting Leist.

"Okay, how about a battle of witts?" Leist proposed.

"What did you have in mind?" Athena asked.

"The mortal game of chess." Leist responded, Athena was so taken aback by Leist's answer she accepted immediately

"Two months, if you're going to learn here you will grow in strength and intellect which means Athena is going to be your teacher, and your training partner will be….Dimension Cutter.

Kronos!" Tobias explained, pulling Kronos from the other side of the portal. Leist followed Athena back to her study. Tobias took three steps in a direction and seemingly disappeared to everyone but Harmonia so she followed.

"Why are you here Tobias?" Harmonia asked, looking to the wooly door.

"Keeping our children alive." Tobias responded, ripping the door out and throwing it aside.

"Tobias, you can't just cut off her hands." Harmonia said, worried following him into the room.

"Sure I can, but that's not what I'm going to do." Tobias said, walking over to Clotho and putting his hands over hers. Rings appeared around each of Clotho's finger tips before fading into them.

"What did you do to me?" Clotho asked, rapidly closing and opening her hands.

"I made it so power would no longer flow through your fingertips, it's a spin on a little trick I picked up from Mikey. Used it on the kids too so they wouldn't end up accidentally killing mortals while they lived on Earth." Tobias said, looking at Harmonia for yet another expression of annoyance at him having yet another ability he hadn't gotten around to showing her.

"Why would you do this?" Clotho asked, trembling in fear.

"I wanted to make sure you didn't get any ideas about snatching up my kids' souls. It would take more than ten times the power of Zeus to even stress those by the way." Tobias explained. The pair returned to the Ashes of Asgard as Chrysafén got to work learning to heal.

Leist and Athena played three games of chess that each lasted one day. Athena won the first, Leist won the second, and the third game was a draw. She accepted him as a student on the spot.

CHAPTER 14

The Fall of the Divine Devil

Foréas remained stuck in the Acropolis, attempting to bash a big enough hole into the pillar for the arrow to fall out but to no avail.

"Ah there you are old friend, I've been looking for you," Heracles said, descending before Foréas and casually pulling the arrow from the pillar.

"Who are you?" Foréas asked, in awe of what the man he watched get accidentally beheaded by the Divine Devil on Mt.Olympus was capable of.

"What do you mean? We've been friends since you were at my knee." Heracles responded, with an air of mild smugness and a slightly less than the gentle grin on his face.

"That's preposterous! Heracles couldn't have handled me if I'd grown up without lifting a finger." Foréas exclaimed, attempting to read Heracles' mind.

"I taught you to do that, do you think I don't know how to defend against it?" Heracles asked as a green glow seeped from his eyes.

"I will find out who you are somehow," Foréas vowed, raising his arm to call Mjolnir. The hammer spun through the air, slapping on contact with his hand. Foréas shrank Mjolnir and a magic circle scanned over it, putting the hammer on a necklace around Foréas' neck. Seeing Foréas do this Heracles couldn't help but snicker as Foréas prepared to leave. Foréas was ready to meet up with Achilles to train in the Mortal Realm for another month.

"You'll know when the Divine Devil knows, speaking of which are you planning on just going to get yourself killed? If not, I have a plan however we will need to wait a while to execute it." Heracles said, counting down from five behind his back.

"I'm listening," Foréas responded, looking back at Heracles.

Two months passed and Leist and Chrysafén are back in new fits. Leist was rocking a suit with a gold tie, his hair was slicked back, brown, and faded into blonde, in response to his attire you could see a slight flaring of Tobias' nostrils. Chrysafén was wearing a black dress under a gold jacket, with a white corset and black shoes with white soles, her hair mirrored Leist's and was in twin tails down to the center of her back then braided down to her tail bone.

"Alright you two have earned a sparring match with me, you win if you can land a hit on me, our match starts when the boulder hits the ground," Tobias said, throwing a magic circle generating a huge boulder. The instant the boulder touched the ground Leist cast a thread of power from his finger to Chrysafén.

"Hello Anointed One, long time no see," Satan said, standing behind the throne of God.

"*Now!*" Leist's voice echoed through Chrysafén's mind. Chrysafén closed her eyes and the pair could see across the entire Realm of the Gods. A clock with no hands appeared in the eye on Leist's forehead and time stopped. Leist charged at Tobias, throwing a punch right in his face but his fist was stopped less than a micrometer away by a blue hand around his neck.

"You are extremely impressive not a single other god or goddess with domain over time could stop it on so grand a scale. Even spaces within dimensions in which time flows differently like Helheim and Purgatory standstill. To be fair it does look like you needed her help though, let's see who's superior." Foréas said, stabbing his thumb through the bottom of Leist's mouth as the flow of time returned to normal. Foréas booted Tobias far away as he stopped himself Tobias looked as a blood lusted Leist began approaching Chrysafén, he tried to get in between his children he was cut off by a punch to the gut from Foréas.

"HARMONIA, THE KIDS!" Tobias cried, helpless as Heracles dropped from the sky with an ax kick to be blocked by Harmonia.

"You can either attempt to deal with me now elsewhere. Or die distracted by your family and I'll just kill them after. Well, the children anyway." Foréas said, ripping Mjolnir from his neck expanding it.

"Are you ready to begin our final battle?" Satan asked, arrogantly.

"Even though angels have never had any of the true power of their creator you have almost as much as I do. Tell me what in my Father's name happened to you?!" Jesus asked angrily.

"The Balance Bringer," Satan said, laughing maniacally.

"Foréas that wretched child, enough talking!" Jesus barked, questioning his father for the first time in the back of his mind before rushing Satan. The fallen angel then transformed into a seven-headed dragon beast with ten horns and let out a huge roar. In response, Jesus used the light of seven stars to slay each of the beast's heads respectively. He then changed again but this time into a serpent in which Jesus would then quickly almost dice Lucifer before he reverted to his fallen angel form.

"FINE! IF YOU WANNA DIE THAT BADLY I'LL BE SURE TO FINISH YOU OFF QUICK! DIMENSION CUTTER!" Tobias howled, two golden rings exploded from his eyes as the light erupted into his irises. Tobias whipped Leist by the hair through the portal and into the Acropolis.

"*I'm already dreading this battle,*" Chrysafén thought to herself. The Bloodlusted Leist then drew his weapon. Leist threw his tonfa up in the air and landed a barrage of powerful strikes knocking Chrysafén to the ground catching his tonfa making an x with them pinning her to the ground with them. Leist proceeded to stomp her stomach five times grinding his foot in the fifth time. Chrysafén tripped him freeing her she then spin-kicked in the neck propelling him away she then used that momentum to start volleying him around stopping with a knee to the gut and chopping to the back of the neck. Leist knocked her to the ground again this time mounting her for a viciously savage ground and pound for what felt like an eternity, every time part of her was erased she would heal herself in a vicious loop.

"This chain is the most powerful weapon forged on Mt.Olympus, as unwavering as the wielder's love and as unbreakable as their heart. Created by the combined efforts of Hephaestus, The Fates, and Aphrodite. One of the few weapons made to apply potentially limitless conceptual power to a physical object, but you might know that if you were Heracles. Spanning millions of miles long not even I could escape this chain's grasp," Harmonia explained, lassoing Heracles with the blinding chain, whipping him around in the air, and dragging him through the ground. She opened her fist and the chain retracted at the speed of light pulling in Heracles almost instantly, tightening her grip once more she thrashed him into the ground. Harmonia carefully but firmly stepped on Heracles' head and wrenched the chain, ripping his head from his body resulting in a 30-second red spray from his neck.

"Satan before I send you to the Omni plane with your daughter and the entirety of the Norse Pantheon, I want you to look into my eyes with fear, knowing that what you see back is the power to justify that fear," Jesus said, with a quiet fury. Before being beheaded Satan started whispering something in Latin. Unbeknownst to anyone under Chrysafén's clothing a black cross appeared on her back.

Chrysafén let out a loud wail and released a huge shockwave sending Leist back. Almost obscured by an amethyst ether. Her pupils had been replaced with upside-down crosses emitting a piercing white light. The gold flame sword in her hand turned that same amethyst color. Leist drew his sword once more separating it back into to tonfa They traded sword strikes in three exchanges then Leist converted his tonfa back into a sword and re-sheathed it. Leaping straight toward Chrysafén delivering a knee square to her forehead air seemed to spray out from the back of her head, and she didn't budge he followed it up with an elbow to the jaw harder than the knee, but again she didn't react he then punched her in the ribs harder than the elbow, once again seemingly no effect. Leist then laid into her with a combination of strikes each one than the last as the shadow coming from her body grew with each. It then absorbed the shadow turning the cross on her back from black to amethyst. Leist went to punch Chrysafén in the face but she swatted it down breaking every bone in his arm. Angered Leist went to knee her in the ribs but she raised her shin and blocked it. Harmonia turned around, wrapping the chain around Leist and it began to spark as if resisting erasure.

"Not even your father could have enough power to even crack this chain," Harmonia said, as a magic circle appeared above her hand, dropping a piece of cake which she forces fed Leist. She dragged her children through a magic circle into Heaven before God. Followed by the green soul that came out of Heracles' body, unbeknownst to them.

"Your children are destroying each other and you can't do anything about it. On top of that, it's all my fault." Foréas said, laughing maniacally. Mjolnir flew into Foréas' hand. Foréas then threw Mjolnir up into the sky "Scarlet Lightning Storm!" he called out, black storm clouds appeared. Mjolnir started falling Tobias then diced it shreds Foréas got right in his face and put his knee through Tobias' head, he then grabbed him the collar slapped him, and backhanded him across the face twice with a maniacal smile on his face. Foréas dropped him as Tobias bit through his tongue and the gold light retreated from his irises into his pupils as they turned into mirrored crosses. Tobias ripped Foréas to the ground by the leg and rained down a flurry of blows, up to 150,000 in the span of a second and the universe was quaking with everyone. Foréas raised his arm, calling Mjolnir hitting Tobias with a space-warping lightning strike to the neck, rattling his nerves and stunning him. Foréas got out from under him winding up a hook aimed for his jaw, Tobias blocked the strike with Ascalon's blade. Foréas chuckled as he followed through with the strike, regenerating around the sword as he rocked Tobias. Foréas knocked him away with Mjolnir ripping Ascalon from his arm in the process. He caught himself and compacted Ascalon. Tobias threw the compacted Ascalon at Foréas, he caught the dagger as Tobias was teleporting to it. "He who lives by the sword," Foréas said under his breath. He managed to expand it. Tobias' heartbeat was then cut off by Ascalon's Blade. "Dies by the sword!" Foréas called out, followed by maniacal laughter.

Chrysafén began to writhe in agony, letting out blood-curdling shrieks as smoke came off her back.

"What's happening?! You're not supposed to be able to feel any pain here?!" Harmonia howled, panic overtaking her face as the chain retracted back into the magic circle on her hand.

"It must be purging some kind of possession or curse," God responded, after five seconds Chrysafén popped right up and began healing Leist.

"Congrats," Tobias said, coughing up a river of scalding blood as the light faded from his eyes.

THE END

www.ingramcontent.com/pod-product-compliance
Lightning Source LLC
Chambersburg PA
CBHW071948190726
48293CB00004B/1401